# The Lost Sorcerer

*Maureen Murrish*

Also by Maureen Murrish

# Chapter One
## *The Power of the Lion*

Tosni threw down the bundle of firewood and lunged toward the rickety ladder. The baby gave a wet, gummy grin and shuffled to the edge of the bed-loft above his head.

'No. Salif, no. Wait!'

Salif gurgled happily holding out a chubby fist, one tiny digit pointing at Tosni. He had one foot on the ladder when Salif toppled over the edge. Terrified, Tosni flung out his arms in a futile effort to catch her. As he did so he felt a sudden and frightening surge of heat. It started deep inside him and erupted from his outstretched hands in a stream of sparkling energy. Salif's headlong fall slowed. Not daring to move Tosni watched, arms outstretched, as the baby, cocooned in dancing lights, drifted to the dirt floor. Once there she crammed a grubby fist into her mouth and lay looking up at him with adoring eyes.

Tosni looked at his hands. Horror at what he had done made his skin prickle. He glanced quickly over his shoulder to be sure he had not been seen. The tiny cottage was empty. The dirt road, visible through the open door, was also deserted. The knot in his stomach eased a little. Pushing aside the fears for himself, he knelt beside the baby and ran his hands over her chubby arms and legs knowing even before he did so that she would be unhurt. This terrifying and unnatural power had only ever done good things.

Up to now, he reminded himself. Up to now.

Salif laughed her stuttering chuckle and Tosni grinned down at her.

'That was a lucky escape, little sister, tomorrow I'll tie you more securely I think. For both our sakes.'

The shabby room was cast into semi-darkness as a figure stepped into the doorway blocking out the morning light. Tosni's relief at Salif's narrow escape evaporated as the shadow slid over them. He ducked and shielding the baby with his body he covered his head with his arms. When the blow came he knew this time Kavnen had used a piece of the discarded firewood. Pain shot up his forearm and into his shoulder.

'Lazy lout. Didn't I tell you to leave the brat abed.' Kavnen's dark eyes were blazing and her tangled mat of dark curls seemed to bristle with anger.

'I did but...' Tosni stopped. He suddenly realized that to explain that Salif was only with him because she had somehow loosened the rope tying her safely in the attic space then fallen from the bed-loft would lead to dangerous questions. He knew only too well what would happen if Kavnen or the villagers suspected he had magic.

'But? But what? She somehow got herself lose and down the ladder so she could help?'

Tosni swallowed, his mouth was dry and he was unable to answer.

'Well?'

'No. I... I brought her down because I thought...I thought...'

'Well don't. Not until you're done working anyway.'

Kavnen looked down at Salif. At the sight of her mother, the baby had stopped gurgling and lay watching her with big solemn eyes. As Kavnen moved

4

closer the baby began a thin wail. Tosni went to comfort her but Kavnen pushed him aside and picked Salif up by the front of her ragged shift. She dumped her on a pile of rags in a corner that was fenced off by an overturned bench. Throwing the piece of firewood at Tosni she snapped, 'Now, clear this lot up and get on.'

Tosni gave Salif a quick, reassuring smile before bending to collect the firewood.

Later, when Kavnen settled down for her usual afternoon nap, Tosni scooped Salif up and went to meet Willem. This was the best time of the day. For an hour or two he would be able to do just as he pleased; as long as it included Salif. That was fine by Tosni, he preferred to keep her where he could be sure she was safe from Kavnen's unpredictable temper. He was particularly eager to get away today as his friend had promised to bring him something important. Willem had been very mysterious and wouldn't say what it was only that it could be vital to their plans. Tosni's breath misted in the cold air as he jogged the remaining way to the stream with Salif bobbing on his hip. Willem was there already.

'What kept you? I've been here ages.'

'Sorry,' Tosni gasped, 'I had to wait until Kavnen was asleep.'

'Still not calling her, mother then?' Willem grinned. It was an old taunt and Tosni shrugged his indifference. As far as he was concerned Kavnen had forfeit the right to be called mother the time she had almost starved him to death.

'Never will either. Anyway I don't really believe she is my mother. How could she be? Look at me. Look at Salif!'

Willem's eyes raked over Tosni's flame-red hair and green eyes to Salif's dark curls and velvety black eyes so like her mother's. He grinned broadly.

'Well that's exactly what I want to show you.' With the air of someone unveiling a priceless jewel Willem took from his shirt a square of yellowed parchment and held it reverently between cupped hands. Folding his lanky frame onto the grass he gently spread the parchment before them and pointed at it.

Tosni put Salif down and squatted next to Willem. He stared at the little black squiggles on the parchment then at Willem's grinning face.

'See?' Willem said, tucking his long brown hair behind his ears.

'Err, no. I can't read, remember?'

'Eh? Oh, yeah, sorry.'

Tosni watched Willem trace the words with a finger in awe at the way he made sense of what were to Tosni infuriatingly indecipherable marks.

'Lord Dunbia and his wife, Lady Metalin, seek their son who was snatched some eleven summers ago. The boy will be approaching his thirteenth summer and is likely to have the red hair of his mother's tribe. The Lord and Lady offer a handsome reward for the safe return of their son.'

'But...?' Tosni began.

'Now do you see?'

'Where did you get this?' Tosni grabbed the parchment turning it over in his hand as if the answer would be on the back.

'I kind of borrowed it from father. He got it when he was selling stuff in Dillant.'

Tosni looked blank.

'You know! Dillant! Where father goes to sell his leather stuff!'

Tosni blinked.

Willem sighed, 'The village a couple of valleys to the west of here? You really have to do something about your knowledge of the country if you're going to stand a chance of finding your parents.'

Tosni's heart fluttered in his chest like a startled animal. 'Find my parents?'

'You're leaving aren't you?'

'Well, yes, I'm planning to take Salif and leave Kavnen but who said anything about...'

'Why do you think I risked having the life beaten out of me by stealing this for you?' Willem said, snatching the parchment back from Tosni. 'It's good parchment! Father was going to use the back to make list of things he has for sale. He'll skin me alive and tan my hide if he finds out I took it!'

Tosni grinned as he absentmindedly pulled Salif away from the water's edge. He knew it was an empty threat. Willem was an only child and his father doted on him.

'Anyway,' Willem continued, 'I think Dillant is the place to start. Father said the Lady had fiery red hair and eyes as green as the metron birds' eggs, just like you. Red hair is really rare, Tosni. It's got to be you they're looking for. It all fits. Father said Kavnen came to the village eleven summers ago when you were one or two summers. I'll bet Kavnen stole you as a kind of...of slave or something,' he shrugged, waving away the unimportant details.

'But even if they are my parents,' Tosni said, 'how am I supposed to find them? Where do they live? Which direction did they take?'

'South,' Willem reported, imitating his father's nasal tones and gesturing wildly, 'to the centre of the world where no self-respecting man would want to be.

Strange and unnatural things go on in the south and a good man is best out on't.'

Tosni's grin at Willem's pantomime faded at the rumour of 'unnatural things' but his voice was steady as he took a chook-size pebble from Salif's fist as it was being pushed into her mouth and asked, 'What kind of unnatural things?' He had the uncomfortable feeling he already knew the answer.

Willem gave a quick look about before whispering, 'Sorcery.'

Tosni couldn't help the sharp look he gave Willem.

'Hey, don't look so worried. I'm sure that won't include your parents. I mean, you're not unnatural are you! And you probably would be if they,' he lowered his voice again, 'were sorcerers.'

Tosni gave him a twisted grin. To give himself time, he took Salif to the edge of the stream and paddled her feet in the water. Salif screamed in delight as the icy stream splashed over her grubby toes. Tosni knew with a certainty that was almost painful that it was time to leave the village. He and Willem were planning it already but time was running out. His magical incidents were becoming more frequent. Willem didn't know the whole reason why Tosni had to leave. But Tosni knew the longer he stayed, the greater the chance someone would find out about his growing powers. As he held the dancing, kicking Salif he realized Willem was right. He should be looking for his parents. If they were sorcerers they would be able to help him. And if they aren't? A small voice in his head argued. And if they aren't I'll worry about it then.

'Well? Willem said, sounding a bit disappointed, 'I thought you'd be pleased. What do you think?'

'I think...' Tosni said swinging Salif back onto his hip and tucking her now pink toes under his jerkin. 'I think you're a genius, Willem. You're right. I need to find my real parents. But it's too early in the season yet. It's too cold for Salif and I don't fancy being out in this either. We'll go in the spring. In the meanwhile we can collect a few things for the journey.'

'Great. I thought you might say that so I've made a start. Here, take this.' He pushed the parchment back to Tosni as he sprang to his feet and bounded over to the old willow. Scrambling beneath its branches he reappeared with a torn blanket, a couple of turnips and a broad grin.

# Chapter Two
*The Treasure*

That evening, Tosni took Salif into the upper space below the rafters where they slept. He went to bed the same time as Salif as he was often so tired he looked forward to sleep and escape from Kavnen. But mostly it was because he wanted to be sure Salif didn't make a fuss and draw Kavnen's attention to her. Kavnen had been particularly irritable today because Halon had still not arrived. For as long as Tosni could remember Halon had visited every forth moon, but it was now six moons since his last visit. He hoped it would not be too much longer before Halon came as Kavnen was growing evermore violent in her frustration. Not that Tosni looked forward to Halon's visits. Each time Halon arrived, Tosni would be paraded for his inspection. Kavnen would fawn over him and pet him while Halon felt his arms and ribs and pulled back his head to inspect his teeth. Satisfied, he would hand Kavnen a bag of coin and leave.

Tosni hated both Halon and Kavnen almost as much as he loved little Salif. From the moment he had helped to bring her from Kavnen's body he had adored her. He had begged and pleaded with Kavnen not to give the baby to widow Cricknal in whose dubious care babies tended to mysteriously disappear. He appealed to Kavnen's greed, telling her if he raised the baby she could then work for Kavnen, maybe even hired out for coin when she was old enough. He was rewarded with the sole task of caring for the infant.

Salif was sitting on his crossed legs with her head against his chest. He leaned forward and kissed the dark curling hair so like her mothers. As he held the wriggling baby he re-lived the horror of her fall from the loft that morning and the terrifying manner of her escape. He remembered the first time he had shown signs of being a sorcerer. He had been locked up in the wood store and starved by Kavnen to the point of death, the finest white bread and spring water materialized before him. His terror hadn't stopped him from cramming the bread into his mouth and washing it down with the sweet water.

And then there was the time she tried to crush his skull with the fire-iron only to fall to the floor in a faint before she could strike.

Up to now his powers had only brought about things he desperately needed. Things that had resulted in good being done. But that could change at any time he knew. It had to change, why else were people so terrified at even the mention of magic. It must turn to something evil. Evil like the demons of the pits. It was said the demons were once magicians and sorcerers whose magic corrupted them until they became shadows of evil. His powers scared him but even more terrifying was the ever present danger that Kavnen or the villagers would find out about them. Three summers ago he had seen what happened to a boy who they suspected of becoming a sorcerer. The boy, who was 13, which as far as Tosni could tell was about the same age as he himself was now, was dragged from his mother's arms and stoned. Then he was bound and thrown into the millpond to drown, or if his powers saved him from drowning, to be eaten by the water demon. Even though it was before Tosni's powers had begun to develop, he had been unable to watch. He ran into the wood and kept running until he could no longer hear the boy's screams and the villagers' howls of fear and anger. He felt ashamed of his cowardice. Not because he was unable to join in with the villagers, but because he left the boy to face his fate alone. He was left with the awful feeling he ought to have done something to help him. He stayed out all that night and at first light he forced himself to go to the millpond. There was no sign of the horror of the day before. The water was still and silent. It was as if it had never happened. As if the boy had never existed. Tosni threw a handful of wildflowers onto the dark waters then returned to Kavnen's dismal cottage and his beating for running off.

He twined a finger into Salif's dark curls. He wished he could share his fears with Willem. He imagined what it would be like to have someone to talk to about it. He sighed. He knew he would never tell Willem. Willem would have to tell the villagers about him or face the same fate as Tosni and Tosni would not risk either happening.

A flash of brightness in the drab loft caught his attention. A dirty rag and cord lay discarded and Salif was cooing in delight at the prize she had unwrapped.

'Hey there little lady, give that here.'

He eased the chubby fingers from the colourful object, careful not to cut them on the jagged edge. The baby wailed her displeasure and he pushed a piece of dried bread into the grasping fist. As Salif ground her gums on the crust the treasure caught and held Tosni's attention. It was half oval in shape. The inner edge was sharp and jagged as if broken away from something. The outer edge was smooth. On the back, in the plain gold-coloured metal, were the marks of the craftsman's tools. But it was the front that made Tosni's heart leap. The red, green and blue enamel glowed in the murky loft. Green hills topped by blue sky and in the foreground the red hindquarters of what he took to be a lion. Tosni stared at it and the familiar sense of longing swept over him. What was the secret of this scrap of broken metal? He had owned it and kept it hidden for as long as he could remember but where had it come from? What was the hold it had over him and why did he feel this overwhelming restlessness when he looked at it?

Salif wriggled impatiently. He wrapped his treasure up but as he was about to push it back under the bed-rushes he hesitated. Instead, he tied it and the parchment he had been given by Willem about his waist with a strip of cloth. Salif whimpered sleepily as he settled her down for the night. Kavnen's sharp voice came through the hatch.

'Keep the brat quite or it'll be the worse for you both, you hear?'

'I hear.'

'I've business to attend to, I'll be back later.'

As Tosni snuggled down next to Salif in the loft, he had no way of knowing that it would be for the last time.

# Chapter Three
*Torn Apart*

He was unable to say how long he had been sleeping when the door crashed open announcing Kavnen's return. Salif wailed her protest at been woken so abruptly and Tosni hastily soothed her.

'Get down here and leave the brat where it is,' Kavnen yelled.

Tosni was more than happy to leave Salif safely in their bed-loft. If the fire-iron was to be used as a weapon again he would rather she was out of harm's way. He stuffed the last of the crust into her ever grasping fist, made sure the rope around her middle was tied securely, then climbed down the shaky ladder to face Kavnen. As soon as he looked at her flushed face and bloodshot eyes he knew he was in for trouble.

Her words slurred together as she said 'I have news of your father that I think might interest you.' Kavnen had always referred to Halon as Tosni's father. Tosni didn't believe it any more than he believed Kavnen was his mother. Thinking it unwise to say so at that moment he stayed silent, waiting for the news he knew could not be good.

'He's dead,' she said brutally.

Truthfully Tosni could not say he was particularly sorry to hear of Halon's death. But he had the distinct feeling Kavnen was about to change that.

'He was killed in a knife fight some three moons ago which would explain his unexplained absence.' She decided this was a great witticism and giggled. Swaying slightly she grabbed the back of the settle to steady herself. 'But that leaves you in somewhat of a pi... a pickle m'boy. You see, I only cared for you out of the goodness of my heart, and the gold I got every fourth moon. In fact, until Halon came along with you tucked under one arm, I had a future. D'you know that?'

Tosni's heart gave a great leap. So he was right; Kavnen wasn't his mother. It was the first time Kavnen had told him anything about his past. She had always refused to discuss it.

Kavnen's bloodshot eyes misted over as she said, 'Back then I was admired and envied by every dancer in the north. I was loved and adored by nobleman and peasant alike. I could twirl and spin like no other.' She lifted her arms above her head in a parody of a twirl and crashed heavily into the mud wall. 'Everybody loved me. Oh I was a beauty. I danced before kings and was pursued by their sons. I had jewels and silks and... and then... and then I met Halon.' A faraway look had come into her bleary eyes. 'He was dashing and charming and promised me the world. He promised me marriage, just imagine that, if you please, a dancing girl, marrying a nobleman. How could I resist him? All he asked of me in return was that I look after his son for a little while. A son he had snatched from the jaws of death. Then, as soon as it was safe, we would be wed.' She slid heavily to the floor tears rolling down her ravaged face, skirts twisted around thick, puffy ankles. 'How could I resist? Tell me that. I would have done anything for him, marriage or no.' she sniffed and her tone changed to one of bitterness. 'So I took you, and I waited. And waited. Even after I found out he was no more a nobleman than I was a queen I still waited.' Kavnen dried her face on the hem of her skirt and heaved herself back to her feet glaring at Tosni. 'And now, here we are. No more Halon. And no more gold.

And I says to myself, 'Kavnen, you can't afford to let your goodness of heart dictate over good sense any longer. You have a weanling to take care of and can't afford to keep someone else's spawn for nothing.' And good advice it is I answer myself, so you got t'go. Now.'

Tosni was still going over what Kavnen had told him, fascinated by this insight into their past. But her last words seeped into his consciousness like cold water.

'What?'

'You heard. Get out. Go.'

'Go where?' Tosni said, hardly able to take in what Kavnen was saying.

'That's your problem, not mine. Out.'

'But it's the middle of the night! In the middle of winter.'

'Out.' Kavnen screamed trying to grab him by the shoulders.

Desperate, Tosni appealed to Kavnen's greed. 'But you need me. I clean for you and, and cook and... ,' he couldn't prevent himself from glancing up to the loft.

A spiteful gleam came into Kavnen's eyes. 'Ah, so that's your game is it? You want to steal my precious daughter from me, eh? Well it'll take more than the chaff in your pockets to prise her from my loving arms. Now go, get out and don't bother coming back. At least, not without gold.'

Tosni didn't move. He felt like the world was closing in on him, crushing him. He was intending to leave, of course he was, but not like this. Not in the middle of the night, in the grip of winter and with nothing but the clothes he stood up in. And not without Salif. As he struggled to take a breath, Kavnen took hold of his arm and dragged him toward the open door. Salif had begun to bawl hysterically. Her obvious panic brought air to Tosni's lungs in a rush. 'No, please, I work hard for you don't I? I'll work twice as hard. I'll hire myself to the penny gang and earn cash. Please.' All the time he pleaded his arms ached to be holding Salif. She needed him. Who would care for her?

But Kavnen was past reason. Enraged at her inability to drag him out of the cottage she took a piece of firewood and brought it down repeatedly on his head and arms. Tosni was forced through the open door.

Realizing his pleas were doing nothing to persuade Kavnen, he took hold of the wildly swinging firewood and looked directly into her bloodshot eyes. 'Keep her safe and I'll be back and bring gold. But if you harm her....'

Kavnen wrenched the firewood out of his grasp and threw it into the darkness. 'I can't swear how long my patience will hold. I suggest you come back soon. But if I see you again and your pockets are still empty, I'll kill her myself.'

# Chapter Four
*Cold Goodbyes*

Tosni stood looking at the closed door. The sound of Salif's cries were muted now but he could still hear her panic. Warm tears rolled down his cheeks. The pain of leaving her threatened to choke him. How was she going to survive without him? Kavnen could hardly bare to touch her. Swiping the tears from his cheeks he turned and walked away. Salif's terrified screams followed him along the icy road. It was the most difficult thing he had ever done but he kept walking. He felt as though he were tearing away part of himself with every step.

The cold bit through his thin shirt and leggings. His bare feet crunched through ice coated mud. He walked blindly with no idea of where he was going or what he was going to do. As he reached the edge of the village, the leather-smith's cottage loomed into view. It was a squat and sturdy stone building, heavily thatched and with two small glazed windows. The image of Willem's cheerful face came into Tosni's mind. What would Willem say when he found out his friend had left without saying goodbye? Tosni stopped and stared at the windows. He stepped out of the icy mud and onto the slippery cobbles surrounding Willem's cottage. Going to the second window he tapped lightly. Almost instantly Willem's face appeared. It was hideously distorted by the coarse glass and Tosni took an involuntary step back. But it was Willem's familiar voice that whispered,

'Who's there?'

'It's me, Tosni.'

Willem's misshapen face pressed against the glass. 'Tosni?'

'I've got to talk to you.'

'Come to the workshop door.'

Willem disappeared and Tosni picked his way around to the side-door where Willem waited for him.

'Come in, quick.'

Tosni stepped gratefully inside. The long, low workroom doubled as Willem's bedroom. The fire was no more than a pile of glowing ash but the warmth trapped within the thick walls was as welcoming as a thick blanket.

'What's wrong? Is Salif sick?'

Tosni shook his head. 'No, she's fine. It's... It's Kavnen, she's put me out. She's found out that Halon's dead and she won't be getting any more money and she put me out.'

'What? I don't understand. What's Halon got to do with it?'

Tosni slumped into the chair by the dying fire and told Willem everything Kavnen had told him.

'But Halon wasn't my father, I know it!' Tosni said through clenched teeth.

''Course not. You're the son of Dunbia, not Halon. That advert says so, doesn't it! But maybe,' Willem said grabbing Tosni's arm, 'maybe he was the one that stole you. An he hid you with Kavnen!'

'Why?' Tosni asked. Willem's theory made no more sense than Kavnen's story did.

'D'know. The important thing is to decide what we do now.'

Tosni noticed the 'we' and was immensely grateful for his friend's support.

'I think we should find that Lord Dunbia who issued the reward poster. It shouldn't be too hard for us to...'

'Us? Willem, you can't come. What about your parents?'

'But...'

'No, I mean it. Besides there's something you can do for me here. I want you to make sure Salif's okay. You know, take her out sometimes and get her medicine if she takes ill; I'll repay you somehow,' he added quickly. 'And make sure she gets plenty to eat? I know it's asking a lot but...'

'Don't worry she'll get half of mine if she has too. It'll be a relief; mother thinks I'm too thin and that I don't eat enough. I'll just cram it into my pocket when she's not looking then give it to Salif. That way everyone will be happy!'

Relief washed over Tosni. 'I'm not going to leave her here with Kavnen any longer than I have to so it won't be forever.'

'What are you going to do?'

Tosni shrugged. 'I'd decided to find my real parents if I could. I'm just going sooner that we thought.'

'But we haven't had time to prepare anything.'

Tosni shuddered as he thought about the freezing weather and his lack of preparation. He wrapped his arms around his thin body. 'Yeah, well. There's nothing I can do about that.' He stared into the hot ashes.

Willem got up and went to a chest near the window. Lifting the lid he pulled out a heavy cloak and a pair of soft boots. The cloak was of heavy broadloom in muted tones of fawn and brown. It was carefully embroidered with the head of an eagle, Willem's birth spirit. The boot's strong leather was worked to suppleness by his father's fingers. Both boots and cloak were lined with rabbit fur.

'Father made these for my thirteenth birthday next month to celebrate my coming of age,' he said hugging the boots to his chest. 'I'm not supposed to know about them. He dropped the boots at Tosni's bare feet. They fell with a soft flump. Then he picked up the cloak fingering the intricate embroidery. 'They've been working on them for weeks. I had to pretend I didn't notice him and mother hiding them whenever I walked in.' He draped the beautiful cloak around Tosni's shoulder.

'Willem, I can't...'

'Oh. I see, so you're just going to curl up and die out there are you? 'Cause that's what's going to happen. You'll never get Salif back that way. Here, take them. You can return them when you come for Salif.'

Tosni pulled the cloak around him. The warmth of the furs seemed to soak into his bones, comforting him.

'Thanks,' he said thickly.

As he laced the long fur-lined boots up his legs, Willem left the room. When he returned he held out a small coarse sack and a handful of coppers.

'I've put some things from the larder in the sack. Not much. A loaf, some cheese and stuff, but it'll help. The coin is mine but you need it more than me.'

Tosni took what was offered and looked at his friend. He wanted to tell him how much this meant to him but his throat felt uncomfortably constricted. He nodded and turned to the door. The cold air rushed into the cottage when Willem pulled it open. Tosni turned for a last look at his friend then stepped out into the biting cold.

By the time he had collected the blanket and turnips from the willow and climbed to the edge of the forest the first light of dawn was showing in the sky. He turned and looked back at the village. At the furthest edge, Kavnen's tiny cottage was just visible through the morning mist.

'I'll get you back, Salif. I promise,' he whispered. Then he turned west into the forest and headed toward Dillant.

# Chapter Five
*Dillant*

It was market day, the streets of Dillant were noisy and crowded. On the cobbled road, riders jostled for position with vendors, beggars and carts. An ornate carriage came bowling along the busy street scattering everyone before it. Tosni was amazed that after it clattered passed there seemed to be no damage. He'd expected overturned carts or a few squashed hens at least. Nor did anyone seem remotely surprised by its breakneck speed.

He was near the centre of the town before he plucked up the courage to approach one of the busy strangers to ask about Lord Dunbia and his visit. As he reached into his shirt for the parchment an old woman slipped on the ice and fell heavily against him. She let out a scream as her basket fell and her meagre purchases scattered over the dirty pavement to be kicked by passing feet. Tosni hastily bent to help her pick up her things and put them into her basket then he handed it back to her.

'I haven't stolen anything!' Tosni said when the old woman checked her belongings while muttering her suspicions.

As the old woman made to walk away Tosni pulled out the piece of parchment with Dunbia's proclamation on it.

'Do you know anything about the Lord and Lady who wrote this proclamation?'

'Don't know nothin' about nothin',' she said sniffing and wiping a reddened nose on a grubby sleeve.

Tosni tried again. 'I just wondered where they...'

The old woman was not listening. She shuffled away and re-joined the flow of people. Tosni watched her disappear into the crowd. After trying several more people none of who showed the least interest in helping him he slumped back against the wall.

'Great, just great!'

A young girl tugged on his cloak. She was no more than six or seven years old. Her clothes were ragged, her hair matted, and a threadbare blanket was pulled tight around her skinny shoulders.

'You askin' about the Lord and Lady what came 'ere a few moons ago? The ones what were looking for their lost babby?'

'Err, yeah, I am. Do you know...?'

'What's it to you? What you want to know for?'

'I want to know where they came from.'

'What's it wurf?'

'What?'

'If I tell you what I know what'll you give me in return?'

The girl's direct manner was unnerving and her guttural accent made her difficult to understand.

Tosni shrugged, 'Nothing, I don't have anything to give.'

'You git noffin for noffin that's what I say.' The girl shrugged and turned away.

Tosni saw the only person willing to help him slipping into the crowd and made up his mind.

'What about this?' He held out the ragged blanket Willem had saved for him.

The girl turned back to him. 'Mebe. Give's it 'ere then.'

'Tell me what you know first.'

A grin split the girl's bony face. 'You made a big mistake not slipping some of that auld woman's things into your pocket but you learns fast. I likes that. Okay, smarty, they went souf.' She held out her skinny hand pointing down the road.

'Souf? Oh, right, I know that already.' Tosni said tucking the blanket back under his arm.

'Patience, I's not finished, is I,' she said her hand now tucked onto her hip. 'They was talking about Harnde. About a castle an all, an about uver stuff I didn't understand. Said they 'ad to get back and that the catchers could `andle things now. You the one they're lookin' for then?'

'Yes. No. I don't know,' Tosni said distractedly.

'Make ya mind up. Anyway, do I get the blanket then or what?'

Tosni held out the blanket then snatched it back.

'What's the catchers?'

The girl put her hands on her hips again. 'Dog's breath, you likes you moneys wurf don' ya? An fancy not knowing who the catchers is. Where you from then?'

'Around,' Tosni said evasively,

'Not around `ere that's for sure. The catchers are the chil'n catchers, you knows, the ones what catch kids like us and sell us to the wild people down souf as slaves. Most of `em have a scar on their cheek, just `ere,' she pointed a dirty finger at her right cheek 'Looks like this.' She drew a crescent moon into the muck on the path, 'If they're caught, see, they's marked, so everyone knows they's catchers.' She shook her matted hair, 'Don't want to get mixed up wiv `em!'

Tosni held out the blanket again and the girl snatched it and ran off with her prize.

25

Tosni watched her go. He was already regretting his impulsiveness. He would be cold tonight. Even colder than he had been the last two nights. But at least now he had the name of what? A town, a land? He looked after the girl wanting to ask what Harnde was but he was too late. She had disappeared into the crowds as if she had never been.

Tosni turned to the rows of stalls set up along the roadside. He supposed he ought to get some more food. He found a stall that offered what looked like food that had passed its best. The bread was hard and unappetizing, the fruit and vegetables wrinkly and the cheese and meat gave off a sour odour. But it was cheap. He bought as much as he could with the money from Willem then left the village and headed south.

Tosni pushed the last meagre scraps of food back into the bag and shuffled deeper beneath the pile of leaves. The light was failing fast and he had learnt over the past five nights that it was wisest to find a safe place to settle down before it became dark. This was his third night since leaving Dillant and he had been right about missing the blanket.

He pulled up the hood of his cloak and blessed Willem again for his generous gifts. Without them he knew he could not have made it this far, he would have died of the cold and Salif would have been left with Kavnen forever. He heard Salif's terrified cries in his mind again and anger at his inability to help her bubbled inside him. Where had his power been when he needed it? Why hadn't he been able to use it to get Salif? But then, he reasoned, she could never have survived the journey in this cold. And at least she had Willem to watch out for her. She would have plenty to eat, he thought as his stomach protested at the meagre rations. Despite the cold and hunger he never doubted he was doing the right thing. The thought of reaching Harnde and finding his parents was a powerful motivator. Over the past five days of hunger and cold he had convinced himself that Dunbia and Metalin were his parents.

He dug beneath his cloak and shirt and pulled out his treasure. This scrap of bright metal was a link to his past. He knew that as clearly as if it had spoken to him. He looked at the colours, subdued now in the failing light. Again the feeling that he was doing the right thing, going the right way soothed him. This was what he was meant to be doing and somehow this colourful treasure was going to help him return to where he belonged.

Five more, cold, torturous days passed. Tosni had used the last of his food bought at Dillant days ago. He kept going by gathering what was left of the shrivelled berries that even the birds would not consider eating. Once he saw a squirrel visiting a nut store. He chased it off and took the small stash of hazelnuts for himself relishing every mouthful. By the time he had stumbled out of the forest on the fifth day he was feeling weak and light-headed. He looked down at the dirt road. It swam before his eyes and he dropped to his knees. Crawling to the other side of the road he curled into the roots of one of the last oak trees before the forest turned to open plain. Dimly he registered the road to his left and the land opening out onto a vast plain to his right before he fell into an exhausted asleep.

He woke to rough hands dragging him out of the roots of the oak. Heart pounding, senses spinning, Tosni struggled to break free but one of the two men gripped

Tosni's upper arm and pulled him to his feet. A third man stood by three horses on the dirt road.

The man holding him growled,' Standstill you little whelp or it'll be the worse for you.'

As the man leaned forward to tie Tosni's hands, an unpleasant blast of tobacco, sweat and foul breath hit Tosni. He gagged and staggered, his queasy stomach protesting, his head spinning.

The man, noticing his reaction grinned. 'Not much fight left in this one. Any longer and he wouldn't have been worth stopping for.'

Tosni's gaze slid from the uneven, rotten teeth to the right cheek where, etched into the black stubble was a dying crescent moon.

Catchers.

# Chapter Six
*Scarface*

The catcher dragged Tosni's arms behind his back and began to tie them. Tosni threw himself backwards in a frantic attempt to break free. But, weak and disorientated, he succeeded only in lurching to one side. It was enough to catch Scarface off guard and he lost his grip on the ropes he was about to secure around Tosni's wrists. Tosni stumbled to his feet and began to run, throwing off the slackened ropes. The second man laughed while Scarface swore loudly. The burst of adrenalin was the fuel Tosni needed and he lunged back across the road and into the forest.

'Got yourselves a wild one there looks like. An' if you're not careful you're going to lose `im,' laughed the third man who was still holding the horses. 'Like a young buck `e is!'

The man with the scar swore again and Tosni heard him thundering after him. He glanced over his shoulder. Both men were following but he was back amongst the trees and tried to use them to shield him from his pursuers. A huge tree, its bole split in two, loomed before him. Tosni leaped inside the wide crack and crouched down, making himself as small as possible while trying to control his ragged breaths. He pulled the hood of his cloak over his head hoping the soft browns and fawns would help to conceal him. He heard the men blundering up to the tree and then pass by. Tosni's heart bounded in his chest like a trapped animal. The catchers' crashing foot falls retreated into the forest. Then they stopped.

'Where'd he go?'

'Back, back we must `ave passed him.'

With a huge effort Tosni forced himself to stay where he was and not bolt from his hiding place in panic.

'He's got to be around here somewhere. You go that way.' Tosni recognized the voice as belonging to the man who had pulled him to his feet, the one he thought of as Scarface. He held his breath as Scarface retraced his steps passed the tree where he was hiding. Scarface had his eyes on the ground as if looking for tracks. He walked almost ten feet passed the tree before he stopped and crouched to the ground. Then slowly he stood up and turned to look straight at Tosni. Tosni's stomach plummeted as a broad grin spread across Scarface's features. Not waiting for what was to come, not even thinking twice, Tosni leaped out of the tree straight at Scarface. He had the satisfaction of seeing the grin turn to alarm before Tosni collided with him and knocked him to the ground. Scarface yelled as Tosni pummelled his chest and head with clenched fists before staggering up and running again. This time though, he got no further than a few steps when the second man crashed out of the bushes on his right and knocked him to the ground. A huge fist ploughed into Tosni's stomach and he curled up gasping for breath. His arms were pulled roughly behind his back and his wrists tied together.

'Wildcat this one,' the second man panted, 'We'll get a good price for 'im if we...'

'Not this time, Dodds,' Scarface gasped wiping the blood from his nose and lip, 'we already got a taker for this one. Have you seen this?'

Scarface pulled back Tosni's hood and grabbed a fistful of hair. 'See this? Sale guaranteed whether or no it's the right one. We can't loose. Otherwise I'd be tempted to give him a bit of his own medicine,' Scarface said as he wiped his blood onto his jacket.

'An' who knows, this might just be the one. He has enough fire in 'is blood that's for sure,' said Dodds as he heaved the still breathless Tosni onto his feet and half pulling half carrying him, started back to the horses. 'An' if it is 'im, don't we get double?'

'Triple, old friend,' Scarface ginned. 'M'Lord and Mighty just don't know it yet.'

They laughed as they crashed back to their companion, dragging Tosni with them.

Tosni was barely able to take in what was being said. He was still winded from Dodds' blow to his stomach. When they came to tie his legs however, he kicked furiously but even had his arms not been tied behind his back he was no match for three grown men. They finished trussing him up then flipped him behind the saddle and over the quarters of one of the horses.

Soon, despite the pain caused by the ropes and the uncomfortable jarring gait of the horse's rump beneath him, Tosni fell into an exhausted sleep.

He woke suddenly when he was thrown to the ground next to a camp fire. Although he could see the thin rim of light from the new day, it was still dark. Dimly he realized he must have ridden all night. Although groggy and ravenously hungry he felt a little better. The rest and the steady heat from the horse's body had revived him a little. He twisted onto his side so he could see. Campfires and tents were all around him. Scarface and his companions were ranged behind him. They didn't speak, they just stood and waited. Satisfied smirks were plastered on all their faces. In front of Tosni was a large, ornate tent. Its canvas was decorated with patterns and shapes in bright colours. Inside were jewel-bright woven carpets covering the sandy soil. Soft shimmering hangings were draped against the walls and golden vessels were filled with flickering light.

The lady seemed to materialize from nowhere into the midst of this light and colour. She was dressed in pale-green robes which swirled around her legs as she moved. Toni's gaze travelled upward to a face full of eager anticipation. Her pale skin was framed by deep chestnut hair. She knelt by his side to lightly touch his hair and he looked into startlingly green eyes.

'Aytasnay? Is it you, at last?'

Tosni barely registered the strange name. He was staring at the woman's hair and eyes. This had to be Lady Metalin, the Lady that Willem's father had described, the one who had issued the reward for the return of their son. The shame of meeting the woman he hoped was his mother while lying in the dirt, bound like a criminal, made his cheeks burn. With the shame came the return of his unpredictable power. Horrified he felt the ropes about his wrists and ankles writhe like snakes and drop away from him. He saw his captors step hastily away, alarmed. He scrambled to his feet and braced himself for the attack. Whatever devilish punishment there was here for the performing of magic he would fight. He would not stop fighting until the last breath was forced from him. Feet apart, fists clenched, his eyes raked the crowd that had gathered around them at a safe distance. Trying to summon his recalcitrant powers, he willed a gap to open in the crowd. Nothing happened. He tried again but this time the lady put herself between him and his chosen escape route.

'It seems we have found you only just in time, your power waxes.' She turned her attention to the guards, 'Bathe him and give him suitable clothes. When he is ready bring him to us. The Lord Dunbia and I have much to discuss with our son.'

# Chapter Seven
### *The Tub*

The guards put Tosni into the care of two serving women. So many thoughts were swirling around in his head he thought it was going to explode. He was astounded by the way these people, these strange colourful people, reacted to his power. Apart from the catchers, they had not shown fear or anger but respect. They did not stone him, but welcome him. He hoped it was proof he really had come home. Dawn was breaking over the camp in earnest now and Tosni stopped to look about. A dozen brightly coloured tents glowed softly in the golden light. People stopped to stare at him. Not in horror, but polite interest. Tosni stared back and they nodded or dipped a curtsy.

'Come, my Lord, don't mind them. I'll take you to your tent and you can refresh yourself.'

Tosni flicked his gaze to the young woman who had spoken. Had she just called him 'Lord'?

The woman smiled and as if she had read his thoughts she said, 'Your mother is Lady Metalin your father Lord Dunbia. You are their son. You are Lord Aytasnay.'

He was a Lord? His cheeks flamed. Of course, had he given it any thought, he would have realised that as the son of a Lord and Lady he automatically would be titled 'Lord'. But the only things on his mind had been escaping persecution for his powers, finding his parents then getting Salif back.

The young woman turned away and he followed automatically. His thoughts drifted back to the woman he had met at the tent. A vague feeling of disappointment leached through him. In the long lonely years in Kavnen's house dreams of escape and finding somewhere he belonged had kept him going. In his wildest dreams he had seen an imaginary mother hugging him and weeping over him, he had seen himself having to disentangle her smothering arms. Maybe, he thought, some memory of her would return, her perfume perhaps, or her smile. Maybe he would even remember some of his life before being stolen. Reality had turned out to be nothing like his dreams. He gave himself a mental shake. She was a Lady, he reminded himself. She would not show her emotions like his imaginary peasant mother. The important thing was he was here. He was home. And soon he would meet his father and then they would get Salif.

Tosni was shown into a curtained off area in a tent almost as grand as that belonging to his mother. In the middle of the floor stood a large wooden tub filled with hot water. Tosni stared at it.

'Come along my Lord. In you get.'

Realization that the maid expected him to strip naked and get into the steaming water made him burn with embarrassment.

He did not move.

'And while you soak,' she continued unperturbed, 'I'll get rid of those filthy, peasant rags and find you something suitable to wear.'

The slur against Willem and his cloak and boots was like a slap in the face. He was exhausted and starving. He had been bound and trussed like a captured deer and slung across a horse's rump to be dumped, humiliated, at his mother's feet. Only Willem had cared. Willem had saved his life by giving him his most treasured possessions. He squeezed the thick cloak beneath his fingers.

'No, you won't!' he snapped, 'You won't touch them, they stay with me. Get out and I'll get into your pool but you will not take these clothes, understand?'

To his surprise and alarm the young woman dropped to the floor, pressing her forehead to the colourful carpet.

'Forgive me. I meant no harm. No one will touch your things my Lord, I swear.' Then she shuffled awkwardly backwards through the curtain.

Tosni stared after her, mouth agape. The girl's response to his outburst of anger brought home to him that he really was a Lord. He was aghast; the last thing he wanted was for people to fall to their knees. He would apologise to the girl next time he saw her. With a last look around to be sure he couldn't be seen he started to undress. He took off the cloak and folded it neatly next to the tub and put his boots on top. He untied the little parcel from his waist containing his treasure and carefully stuffed it into one of his boots. The thought that he would soon find the answers to what his treasure really was made his stomach leap with excitement. He saw himself holding it out to his mother and father. He imagined them laughing, amazed the way he had cared for it all these years. He would tell them how it had always comforted him, how it had helped him through the worst times. Then they would tell him the story behind it and how it came to be with him and why it was so special.

He grinned and peeled off the filthy shirt and leggings and climbed, with difficulty, into the tub. He curled up and sank into the hot water until it came up to his neck and sighed with pleasure. He had never experience anything like it before but, he decided, he definitely would again.

He was immensely embarrassed when the young woman came back while he was still in the tub. Determined not to frighten her again he waited to see what she would do. Cutting a wide berth around his clothes, working quickly and silently, the young woman laid a pair of heavy breaches and a white linen shirt on a chair and draped a green velvet cloak over the back of it. Then she approached the tub.

'Whoa, just stay right there,' Tosni said in panic, trying to keep his voice level and hoping she wasn't going to collapse again. 'What do you want?'

'Why, to scrub you clean of course.'

Tosni felt his face grow hot. 'Well I've already done that, thanks.'

She held up a brownish block of soap and a cloth. This time her eyes held a mischievous twinkle as she said, 'Without these?'

'Well just, just throw them over then.'

The soap and cloth splashed into the water and he gave a weak smile as the young woman dropped the drying cloth onto the floor, bowed then retreated through the curtain. He heard her and a companion giggling as they left the tent.

'Huh! So much for respect,' he muttered.

After his bath Tosni tied his treasure around his waist and dressed in his new clothes. He rubbed his hand over the crisp white shirt and the soft wool breaches. He had never felt anything like it. Within a few minutes the two young women came back into the tent and curtsied. Their eyes were bright and admiring.

'I'm Elena,' said the girl who had brought him the clean clothes and soap, 'and this is Hedna. We are to be your servants, my Lord.'

Tosni judged that by their earlier giggles Elena was over her fright enough for him to say carefully, 'Thanks, Elena, but I don't need any servants. I can take care of myself.'

Elena and Hedna giggled again. 'You're the son of the Lord and Lady, of course you need servants. We've been sent by your mother to take care of you,' Elena said. She swept the fair hair back from her face and continued. 'I'm to take you to dine with your parents but first I must tie back your hair.'

'My hair?'

'You can't dine with the Lord and Lady with your hair all loose like that. Here, I've brought a leather thong, let me tie it for you.'

Elena swiftly and gently tied back Tosni's hair. When she had done, Hedna held up a mirror for him to see himself. He was startled by his reflection. His skin, clean for once was pale and his vivid green eyes mirrored the colour of his cloak. Elena had pulled back his hair into the leather thong and it hung down his back in a heavy braid.

'I hadn't realized how much you look like your Lady mother,' Elena said studying him.

'You're very handsome,' Hedna giggled.

Tosni felt himself grow hot again. He had never blushed so much in his life and decided Elena must think him very stupid. The thought did nothing for his confidence, or his blushing.

'Well, now you're ready, we can take you to the Lord and Lady.'

Tosni took a deep breath to still the butterflies in his stomach then followed Elena and Hedna out of the tent.

# Chapter Eight
*Questions without Answers*

Elena and Hedna led Tosni back to his mother's tent. His insides were squirming with a mixture of nerves and excitement. For most of his life he had wondered what his real parents were like and why he had been separated from them. He would soon have the answers.

The dark haired, dark eyed Hedna stayed at the door of the huge, ornate tent where he had first met his mother. Elena led him inside and pulling aside a decorative curtain she motioned Tosni to follow. She turned and curtsied deeply. Tosni quickly scanned the room. His mother stepped from a shadowy corner.

'Welcome, Aytasnay.'

Before he could answer another curtain was pulled roughly aside and a man strode through it. He was tall and his black hair was pulled back into a braid similar to that which Elena had put in Tosni's hair. He stared at Tosni. His face was eager, his stare intense. Tosni lifted his chin, determined not to show how intimidated he felt at the man's scrutiny. It took all his resolve not to step backwards when the man strode rapidly across the room and seized him by the shoulders. Tosni stared into grey eyes which were searching his face eagerly.

Lady Metalin stepped forward, 'Dunbia, please, you'll unnerve the boy. Show a little restraint.'

Dunbia released him abruptly and stepped back.

'Aytasnay, may I introduce Lord Dunbia Matanza, your father.'

40

Tosni stared at Dunbia then remembering his manners he bowed his head and said, 'I am honoured to meet you… father. I have waited a long time.'

'Too long, Aytasnay, we have a lot of questions, as must you. We can talk over our meal. Come,' Dunbia's voice was eager and loud and in it Tosni imagined he could hear Dunbia's delight at his return.

His mother led them to the heavily laden table. Tosni's feet faltered. He had never seen so much food in his life. Much of it he couldn't put a name to. But he saw sucking pig, duck, rabbit, and what he guessed to be a haunch of venison. There was even a pheasant still wearing its feathers. Fruits and vegetables were heaped up in great piles. Soft bread and creamy cheeses filled the gaps.

Tosni's mouth watered and he felt faint with his retuning hunger.

Metalin smiled at him, 'We don't eat this way every morning, Aytasnay, but then it is not every morning our lost son is returned to us. Come, eat, and when you are ready, we can talk.'

Elena, who had stood quietly by, removed his cloak and Tosni sat at the laden table. For a long while he could concentrate on nothing but the food. When his hunger finally began to be satisfied he realized his mother and father were watching him. His mother wore a half smile while his father's face was intent, his eyes fixed on Tosni's face. Tosni found his father's intense stare unsettling. He stopped eating and laid down his fork.

'Now we can talk. What would you ask first?' his father asked.

The questions chased each other around in Tosni's head. He was as surprised as the Lord and Lady seemed to be when he asked, 'Why did you send child-thieves to catch me?' The words had tumbled out of his mouth unbidden.

His mother's smile faltered then she said, 'First, you must understand how desperate we were to find you. We asked the child-catchers to bring to us any child who could be you. We were terrified you would be sold as a slave and lost to us forever.'

Tosni picked up his fork and stirred it around his plate. 'What about the others? The ones that turned out not to be me? What happened to them? Did you give them back to the thieves?'

A look passed between Lord Dunbia and his wife before Metalin said, 'No! We could never send a child into slavery. We fed them and let them go. They were grateful. And courteous,' she added pointedly. 'Do you not have other questions?'

His head buzzed with questions. His hand tightened on the little pouch at his waist.

'Who am I?'

Lady Metalin smiled, 'You are Aytasnay Matanza of Harnde. You are of the Harndue tribe and you are our son. You were stolen from your crib when you were little more than two summers. We have being searching for you ever since.'

'Who stole me and why?'

'You were stolen by a tribe known as the Pirous. Their leader, their king, is my brother. He is a wicked, evil man. We have been at war with him many years. When you were born it was foretold you would have great power. It is your destiny to end the war between the Harndue tribe and the evil Pirous once and for all.'

Dunbia cut in saying, 'The Pirous heard of the prophesy and stole you, no doubt in a foolhardy attempt to turn you against your people and in doing so, turn your powers to evil. That, undoubtedly, is the only reason they kept you alive.'

Tosni stared at them. 'I was stolen because I would become...' he was about to say a sorcerer but didn't know how these people would react to the term so he finished, 'I mean... because I was going to have powers? I don't understand. Where I lived, with Kavnen, these powers would have got me killed if anyone found out I had them. Now you're telling me I was stolen and kept alive just because someone thought I might have them?'

'There was no doubt you would have them,' Dunbia said, leaning across the table. 'And yes, you would be worth stealing and caring for until you came into your power. And now you are back with us you will fulfil your destiny by killing the Pirous King and ending this war.'

Tosni was aghast, he looked from his father's eager face to that of his smiling mother,

'I can't end your war for you! For a start my powers don't work when I want them to. And I certainly couldn't kill anyone with them.'

'Ha. That will be remedied with training. And training is something you will get plenty of. Everything depends on it.'

Tosni was beginning to feel annoyed, frustrated. Dunbia was not listening.

'You don't understand! My powers have only ever protected me and Sa....' He broke off then said more calmly. 'Lord, my powers aren't strong enough to destroy armies and Kings, even if I wanted them to. Which I don't! There's been a mistake! I'm not the person you think I am.'

Dunbia threw down his fork, 'Can you look into your mother's face and say that? Can you deny the bond of blood? You are so much like her that when I look at you it is like looking at her shade. Denying your heritage is impossible!'

Tosni looked at his mother's serene face. Her heavy red hair, the exact shade as his own, was pulled back from her face exposing her slightly flushed, white skin. Her green eyes were wide and anxious. His heart thumped uncomfortably. Before he could speak his father continued.

'Your powers are only now developing. You will be taught how to weld them and you will become one of the most powerful sorcerers ever known. Your mother tells me your powers are waxing. The sooner you start your instruction the better. There is much for you to learn before we face the Pirous.'

Tosni's annoyance turned to anger. Was that all he meant to them? Was he just a tool they thought they could use to end a stupid war he had never even heard of until today? Was that why he had fought to survive Kavnen's neglect; just so they could turn him into a weapon of war?

'Powerful?' he shouted, 'I suppose that's why I ended up being beaten and starved by Kavnen? And why Halon would come and inspect me as if I were some beast? Why I was thrown out to die when Halon was killed? Why I had to leave Salif behind? If the only reason you want me back is because you think I can kill your enemies for you then you are going to be disappointed. Because even if I could, I wouldn't do it. You may as well give me back to the catchers right now.'

Dunbia banged his fist onto the table making the dishes rattle but Metalin held up her hand as if to calm him. 'We want you back because you are our son and are precious to us,' she said. 'We have no way of knowing why the Pirous held you in the conditions they did but we are grateful to this Kavnen for keeping you alive, she will be rewarded.'

If she thought that this would calm Tosni she was wrong. Tosni jumped to his feet and glared across the table at her, 'You want to reward Kavnen? If you intend to reward anyone then reward Salif; save her from Kavnen. A baby deserves better than to have Kavnen for a mother. You should be helping me save Salif not rewarding Kavnen for her cruelty.'

'Then we shall send for the child,' his father said standing up so abruptly his chair was thrown to the floor. 'But in return I expect you to show better manners. The child will be sent for as you wish but the woman who raised you will be recompensed.'

Breathing hard Tosni glared at his father.

'Are there any other questions, Aytasnay?' Metalin asked.

Tosni hesitated then released the hold he had on his treasure. 'No. None.'

'Then go and prepare for the journey,' his father snapped. 'We return to Harnde, we have been away too long. Lessons in the use of your powers will begin while we travel.' Dunbia turned and kicking aside the overturned chair, he left.

# Chapter Nine
*The Lessons Begin*

Tosni brushed past the anxious Elena who stood waiting for him, and stormed back to his tent. He pulled aside the hangings until he was back in the screened inner quarters. Neither Elena nor Hedna followed him.

Furious, he paced backward and forward. 'They want me to end their war. That's all I meant to them. It's the only reason they want me back. Well I won't do it. They can go find someone else to kill for them.'

He flung himself into a chair. Why hadn't his parents turned out to be ordinary people? Why did they have to be nobility, and what was worse they were nobility on the brink of war! But they do want you, a small voice in his head said, and they are sending for Salif. They didn't have to but are doing it to please you. He got up and went to a small table and picked up the comb Elena had used on his hair twirling it in his fingers. He was missing Salif, he decided. As soon as she was safely with him everything would be fine.

By late morning the camp was disbanded and they began the journey to Harnde castle. Once it was discovered that Tosni could no more ride the fiery young colt he had been brought than he could fly like a bird he was put into the open wagon with the youngest children. The colt was led away tossing his head as if in derision. Tosni's face reddened as the youngsters giggled.

Meals were eaten on the road and as the meagre allowance was handed out for lunch his father rode up to him on a big grey horse.

'Aytasnay, this is Raven,' he said indicating the man with him. 'He is going to teach you to master your powers. But it can't be done from the bed of the children's wagon. You must first learn to ride.' Without waiting for a response Dunbia rode away leaving Raven with Tosni.

Tosni stared at the man. Every inch of the dark skin on show, including his bald head, was covered in tattoos. Eyes, black as coal, stared out at him from swirling lines which spread out from his cheeks to cover his whole face. Huge, intricately patterned hands gripped the reins of his mount and the lead rein of a skewbald pony.

'Get down from there. Your lessons begin.' Raven's voice was a hash rasp very like that of the bird he was named after.

No longer hungry, Tosni handed what was left of his meal to the wide eyed child next to him and jumped from the moving wagon.

Raven wound his way to the side of the road and Tosni, reluctantly followed. True this pony looked far more amiable than the last, but the only horse Tosni had seen before he left the village was the old mare Willem's father used to pull his cart. The thought of actually climbing on board her had never crossed Tosni's mind. He stood at the side of the road not knowing which to keep an eye on; the huge stern faced man or the sad looking little pony.

Raven slipped from his horse's back and stood before Tosni in one graceful movement. 'Ever ridden before?'

Tosni shook his head.

Raven took a step over to him and hoisted him, as if he weighed no more than a baby, into the saddle on the ponies back.

'Well, now you have. Keep your legs down and hold these, he said thrusting the reins in Tosni's hands. Pull the right to turn right the left to turn left and kick it to go faster. Easy as that. So, now you can ride and we can get down to the real lessons.' He undid the lead rein.

'Err, how do I stop it?'

'It'll stop when the rest of us stop. That's all you need to know.' Raven vaulted from the ground back onto his massive black horse and moved away. The pony followed.

Tosni looked down at the ground passing beneath the pony's legs and instantly wished he hadn't. He swayed dizzily and clutched the front of the saddle for support. He decided it was safer to look between the ponies drooping ears and ignore the passing scenery.

'Now, tell me what powers you have shown.'

Tosni looked up at Raven then because it threw him off balance again he looked back between his pony's ears. He still found it strange to be speaking so openly about his powers when even a hint of them would have gotten him killed back at the village.

'Well it started when Kavnen, that was my foster mother, tried to starve me.' Tosni told him how just in time bread and water and appeared. He told him about Kavnen falling to the floor as she was about to beat him with the poker. Then he told him how Salif had been saved by an orb of sparkling light when she had fallen from the loft.

'Your mother told me you loosened the child catchers' ropes when you lay at her feet.'

'Oh yeah, that as well.'

'How did they catch you?'

Tosni began to tell the story of how the child-thieves had chased him into the forest.

'No. I mean why did you let it happen?'

'I didn't have a lot of choice!' Tosni said. Did Raven think he wanted to be caught? 'I tried to run but...'

'I mean why didn't you use your power to stop them?'

'It doesn't work like that. I can't use it at will, it comes and goes as it likes.'

'Not good enough, boy. From now on it will be at your command not the other way around.'

'But...'

'No 'buts', that is your father's order. And you, like us all, will obey.'

Tosni didn't answer. It was all very well saying 'you will obey'. But how on earth was he supposed to do it?

'As it was foretold, it seems you have more than one power. Which of those did you feel was the most powerful?'

'Err...'

'We will work on your ability to change time, as when you saved the child. That seems the most advanced.'

'Change time?'

'You slowed time around the child as it fell, that's how you slowed her fall.'

'But...'

'You must learn not to question me, Aytasnay.'

Tosni was feeling more than a little irritated. 'First, don't call me Aytasnay. My name is Tosni. Second if I don't question then how can I learn? And third who are you, and how do you know all this?'

'A grin split Raven's features. 'So you do have some fire! I was beginning to think you were no more than a pale imitation of your father. Very well, *Tosni*, I will answer your questions. This time. I am The Raven, the Lord's Sorcerer. And I know about magic because I was born to it just as you were. But that is where our likeness ends. You are the son of a Lord, I of a servant. You were raised by a people who feared magic, I by a people who revere it. I was trained to use and enhance my skills from an early age. Until recently, you didn't even know you had powers and your environment has taught you to suppress them. My skills are impressive. Yours will be monumental.'

'Monumental?'

'Greater than any wizard or sorcerer alive. All you have to do is learn how to control them. And so for your first lesson.'

Before Tosni realized what he was doing Raven leaned over and cracked the pony hard on the rump with his whip. The pony threw its head back, screamed in pain and fright then leaped forward and galloped down the grassy edge of the road. Terrified Tosni gripped the saddle with his hands and legs but the harder he gripped the more he bounced around. He hung on with every ounce of strength he could muster but he was becoming more and more unbalanced with every forward lunge of the pony's desperate flight. He knew it was only a matter of time before he fell, he was slipping sideward and he could feel the saddle beginning to slip around with him. This was it, he was going to fall beneath the pony's thrashing hooves and die. The ground was getting closer and closer. Suddenly he felt the familiar rush of power in his stomach. Light sparkled around him and the pony's headlong flight slowed as if it were running through deep mud. Each stride took longer and longer to complete until the pony was still. Tosni, unable to hold on a second longer, slipped off and landed hard on the ground. He rolled away and bounced to his feet staring at the pony. It was frozen in mid-flight, nostrils flared, ears flat against its head, looking like a living statue. Its legs were arced under its body, ready for its next forward lunge, its mane and tail streamed out behind it. The same lights that had surrounded Salif when she fell from the hatch now surrounded the pony and Tosni. He was aware of the curious stares of the party as it passed by on the road, the sound of Raven's plunging horse nearby, but inside the sphere of dancing lights all was peace and stillness. Tosni stepped back out of the sparkling lights and instantly the world returned to normal. The pony completed its stride and galloped madly away. Raven whistled a shrill note and the pony slowed and stopped. Turning around it cantered back to them sides heaving.

'Tosni, white faced and feeling sick yelled up at Raven, 'Are you mad? Why did you do that?'

'To give you some idea of what you are capable of. Soon you will learn to fear nothing. You will discover you can conquer anything. All you have to do is learn to use your power before it becomes a matter of life and death. I, The Mighty Raven, will teach you how to do that. You are fortunate for there is no greater teacher anywhere. Be pleased. This has been only the first of many such lessons.

Tosni stared in disbelief as Raven sat astride his horse, arms crossed on his massive chest and a proud smile on his face. He was about to object, to tell Raven he was not going to play his stupid games but Raven turned to stare at him. Tosni saw behind the self-satisfied expression and into Raven's heart and knew instantly it would be wiser not to cross him.

At least not yet.

# Chapter Ten

*A Mutual Lesson*

It took six days of painful riding for them to reach the castle of Harnde. At noon on the seventh day the company climbed a low rise and looked out onto Harnde. A plain stretched out before them until, directly opposite, it nudged a steep cliff face towering above it. The castle clung to the ragged cliff as if held there by sorcery alone. There were hundreds of windows, dozens of towers all built of dull grey stone like the dull grey of the cliff face they sprawled across. Below it, at ground level, was a huddle of grey houses. A wall arched out from the cliff and back again as if jealously hugging the houses inside closer to the mountain and its castle. Guards were pacing back and forth along its broad top. Tosni stared open mouthed, his aches and pains forgotten. He had never imagined it would look so intimidating.

His father rode up beside him. 'Welcome to Harnde, Aytasnay. The plains below the castle will be your classroom while the castle will be your home.'

Tosni's gaze slipped to the plains at the foot of the granite cliff beyond the castle wall. A huge area had been enclosed by a second wall and its interior was carved into rough rectangles. It was clear to see this second wall was designed more as a boundary for straying livestock than for defence.

At the sight of the company appearing on the rise, a trumpet sounded from the castle. Flags, coloured black and yellow, were run up all over the city to welcome the Lord's return.

Over the next few weeks Tosni discovered that his father had been wrong about one thing; not all his lessons were to be conducted on the plain. As soon as Tosni's inability to read came to Raven's attention he dumped him unceremoniously into the reading class. Tosni's mortification at been put in with children half his age was overridden by his joy in learning to read. He learned quickly and read every chance he got, everything he could get his hands on.

He sat, an open book on his lap, on the window-sill in his room high up in the castle and looked out over the boundary wall, the extent of his world now, toward the north and Salif. It had been almost three moons since he had met with his mother and father and there was still no sign of Salif being brought to him. He rarely saw his parents and each time he did he asked them about Salif. They always said the same thing, 'Patience, Aytasnay, these things take time.' Tosni couldn't understand how it could possible take so long. He had told them where the village was. They had only to show Kavnen the gold and she would be more than willing to give them Salif. He had been told that men had gone for Salif the same day everyone else had started their journey back to the castle. He had given them Willem's cloak and boots to return to him. He wished he could have written Willem a letter. He could now of course but who would take it?

He closed the book and took out the piece of parchment and coloured metal from the pouch at his waist. The enamelled colours were as bright as ever and flashed in the afternoon sun. He traced the shape of the green hills then the blue of the sky then the red hindquarters of the lion. He had never shown his treasure to his parents and as time went by it became almost as unthinkable as showing it to Kavnen. He tucked it back into his pouch and smoothed out the faded scrap of parchment that Willem had given him. Slowly he read the words aloud imagining the look on Willem's face if he could hear him. He grinned at the thought of Willem's long bony face lengthening still further into a look of surprise.

Tosni missed his friend. He missed the friendship they had shared. Though there were other boys at the castle he could talk to it seemed no one was willing to get too friendly with him. They answered any questions he had with the shortest of answers and avoided awkward questions all together. He often heard them whispering together, almost fearfully, as he passed. He supposed it was because he was Dunbia's son. He had been around long enough to know it was not the fact he was a sorcerer that they feared. Though powers such as his were rare, he had learnt, many people had at least magic enough for simple tricks. Magic was as natural as breathing for the Harndue and apparently for the Pirous too. But, most of all, even more than Willem he missed Salif. Her absence was like an open wound which ached constantly.

He stared through the open window across the plains to the forest beyond and for the hundredth time he wondered how things would be had he not been stolen as a baby. Perhaps those open plains would hold more pleasant memories for him than those disturbing ones provided by Raven. Would he of been allowed to play there with other children? Would he have made a friend like Willem? His thoughts were interrupted by a knock on the door. Puffing slightly, Hedna staggered in carrying a pile of books. Tosni pushed the parchment and fragment of enamelled metal back into his pouch and jumped down to help her.

Taking the heavy books from her he said, 'Hedna, the day I was stolen, where was I?'

'What ever do you mean 'where was you'?' she asked, making a show of straightening her skirt.

Since that time in the bath tent, Tosni had been careful not to scare Hedna or Elena again. Slowly they had become more relaxed around him, at least when he was alone. Tosni was glad. With the trust came a companionable respect and a tentative friendship which he was only to aware his parents would not approve of.

'I mean where about in the castle was I. Who was looking after me?'

'What on earth do you want to know that for?' Hedna looked suspicious.

Tosni shrugged 'I'm not trying to get anyone in trouble or anything. I'm just trying to picture it that's all. What happened after father realized I was taken? Did he go after me?'

'What father wouldn't? What a question! You'd best forget all about that and concentrate on your lessons instead. They say that heathen's army isn't too far from being at the gates and your father's expecting you to send them off with a flea in their ear. Anyways, Elena found some books she thought you might find interesting; you've just about read the library dry! Now I got to go, Elena's waiting.'

Hedna slipped through the door and Tosni picked up one of the books and flipped through it. It looked a bit difficult but that was part of the fun. He looked forward to trying out his reading skills later but now he had to meet Raven. He dropped the book onto the bed and left the room.

Raven was waiting for him in one of the rectangles of green laid out before the castle. As Tosni approached him his heart sank. Behind Raven, and held in a cage so tight that it could do no more than toss its wickedly horned head, was a bull.

'At last. I almost came to look for you. And believe me you would not want that.'

Tosni believed him.

'Today you see we have no weapons; nothing but the power you were given. And with those powers I want you to do battle with the bull.'

Tosni's stomach churned. Not again. He knew it was no good appealing to Raven. He had had to kill before but never something as large as a bull. It wasn't the size of the creature that worried him; he had enough confidence in his abilities now to know he could kill it before it got anywhere near him. It was the act of killing he detested. Raven knew both these things as well as Tosni did. The first animal he had been put to had been a wild boar. He was so disturbed at the thought of having to take its life he had merely rendered it unconscious and hoped Raven would not notice. When Raven had approached it and said he was going to skin it Tosni hastily confessed to what he had done. Raven, far from been angry had laughed heartily and stuck the knife into the pig's belly. Sickened Tosni raised his hand and instantly killed the screaming pig. Then he vomited. He never made the mistake of leaving an animal alive again. When given one to kill he did it as swiftly and painlessly as possible. And although he still felt ill when he did it, he had at least gotten the nausea under control.

Tosni eyed the bull. It was in the prime of life. Muscles rippled under its gleaming black coat. Horns, almost two foot long, swept out from each side of its head like scimitars. As he watched, servants standing on the top of the cage, pulled open the door. The bull bounded out and pranced once around the enclosure before casting his angry eyes over to Tosni.

'Why?' Tosni shouted. 'Why make me do it again? You know I can do it. Why again?' The only thing Raven seemed interested in Tosni using his powers for was destruction. Tosni constantly reminded himself that it was natural for Dunbia to want him taught such things when war was so close. But it didn't stop the nagging worry that the villagers where he had lived with Kavnen were right and that Sorcery always turned to evil.

'Why not?' Raven laughed, 'And besides, it has been chosen to grace Lord Dunbia's table tonight. Just picture it as the King of the Pirous. That always seems to make it easier for you. Imagine he is coming to take you away again, back to the hovel you once lived in. Remember that?' Raven waved his hand and Tosni saw looming up before him Kavnen's dingy cottage with Kavnen standing in the doorway beckoning him.

The blood pounded in Tosni's ears but Raven had used this taunt once too often. He shrugged off Raven's spell. The image of the cottage disappeared and in its place he saw the magnificent black bull pawing the ground and tossing its deadly horns. Tosni knew that left to his own devises he could deal with the bull in many ways none of which would be fatal but he wasn't going to leave him to the jeering crowd which always seemed to congregate for his lessons. Besides it would give him great pleasure to outsmart Raven. Raven had told him once that Tosni's powers were far greater than his own. 'Well let's see if that's true,' Tosni thought. The bull began his charge. Tosni brought into his mind a picture of a valley. As he did so he deliberately blocked out Ravens probing thoughts. Then in the valley he put the image of the rapidly approaching bull. He heard the shout of Raven at his shoulder demanding to know what he was doing. Tosni ignored him. As soon as he could picture the bull charging down the valley as clearly as he could see him charging across the paddock, he raised his arm and flicked his hand in the direction of the bull as if swiping away a troublesome fly. The bull vanished. Tosni had a brief glimpse of it skidding to a halt in the valley and spinning around in confusion. Then the picture faded.

Raven grabbed him by the shoulder and spun him around. 'What have you done,' he demanded.

'Denied my Lord his supper!' Tosni said pulling himself free and feeling more than a little pleased with himself. The look on Raven's face was worth what he knew would be coming in the next few days. Tosni faced the angry sorcerer unflinchingly knowing that soon, Raven would have nothing more to teach, and then their roles would be reversed. And when Tosni looked into Raven's eyes he saw that Raven knew it too.

# Chapter Eleven
*Ancient Wisdom*

Tosni returned to the castle feeling happier than he had in a long time. Never again would he be forced to kill for sport. Even Raven's anger could not dampen his relief. He thought back to Raven's first brutal lesson when Tosni had frozen the bolting pony. Raven had said then that Tosni would come to fear nothing, that he would learn he could conquer anything. Well, he had been partially right; Tosni had conquered his fear of Raven. He was pondering this new feeling when Elena hurtled around the corner and ran into him.

'Oomph! There you are!' she panted. 'The Lord Dunbia sent me to look for you ages ago. He wants to speak with you. He's waiting in his room.'

Tosni raised his eyebrows in surprise. His father had never asked to see him in all the time he had been at the castle. 'Why? Is something wrong?'

'Master Tosni! As if Lord Dunbia would discuss that with me! But I do know he hates being kept waiting so stop wasting time and follow, quick!'

Tosni followed Elena as she hurried back through the castle. He had never been to his parent's rooms before and had no idea where they were. Elena eventually stopped outside ornate white doors. She gave a nervous twitch to her skirt smothered her fair hair and after a critical glace at Tosni's hair and jerkin she swung open the doors.

His father paced up and down the spacious room hands on hips. His mother sat sedately before a massive carved fireplace. The mild weather meant the fireplace was empty and cold. A series of arched windows along one wall allowed the sun to pour into the room bringing warmth and light. Elena dropped a curtsy and his father spun around to face them. He glowered at Elena.

'Where on earth...?'

'I was with Raven, father, I've just returned to the castle.'

Dunbia's eyes flicked to Tosni then back to Elena.

'Out!'

Elena turned and ran from the room flashing Tosni a quick grateful smile as she passed.

Dunbia pulled a dark wood chair forward and motioned Tosni to sit. Tosni perched on the edge of the chair. He looked at his mother hoping to find a hint of what this was about. The sun lit her face and hair but her soft smile gave nothing away. His father sat in the chair opposite her.

'How are your lessons with Raven progressing?' he asked abruptly.

'They are progressing well, I think.' Tosni had no intention of telling him about the bull. He was quite happy for Raven to break the news that Dunbia was to go without his chosen meal.

'Good. Nothing is more important than your skill as a sorcerer now. You must practice every chance you get.' He got up and began his pacing again. 'Word has come to us that the Pirous are on the move. They are marching west and should be here within the next few days.' Dunbia stood before the windows putting his face in darkness. 'You have been here almost three moons now. What do you think of your people?'

Truth was Tosni had had little time to meet the people of the city. Raven worked him hard. When he was not learning to control his powers, he was learning to control the fiery little thoroughbred Raven insisted he rode. Then, while indoors, he could not tear himself away from the books he was learning to love. 'I... I like them well enough,' he said.

His answer seemed to satisfy Dunbia who said, 'Yes. The Harndue are a noble people. And they have yielded to the Pirous for too long. The time has come for things to change. Soon the Pirous army will stand at our gates making more demands and you must destroy it. Only then will the Harndue be free.'

'Destroy it?' Tosni repeated. 'Destroy the whole army. I thought it was the king...'

'Our hopes are pinned on you, Tosni,' his mother said. 'The Pirous have long wanted to turn the Harndue into slaves. They will not rest until our army is defeated. I know. Remember, Tosni, I was once a Pirous. Their King is my brother. I saw what they were from the start. But I escaped. I came to the Harndue as soon as a chance arose.'

His father went to stand at Metalin's side and Tosni looked from one to the other. 'But... I can't... I mean I don't want...'

'You don't want? You don't want to... what?' growled his father, 'Help your people? Save your mother? For there will be no mercy for her. She is a traitor as far as the Pirous are concerned.'

Metalin put a gentle hand on Dunbia's arm as she spoke. 'You are the only one with the power to free the Harndue from the threat of the Pirous, Aytasnay. It is the task you were born for. Listen to your father and understand.'

Tosni looked down at his hands. All the pleasure he had felt at outsmarting Raven had evaporated. He was sickened at what his parents were asking of him. Did they really expect him to go out and destroy a whole army? The trick he had played with the bull would not help him this time.

'Is there no other way? Perhaps if they knew that we could defend ourselves now, they would...'

'You were born to destroy them, Aytasnay, whether you like it or not,' his father roared. 'It is your destiny.' He shook off Metalin's restraining hand and began his pacing again. 'You were born for this task. You will destroy their armies. You will use your power to lay them to waste and end their ruling line. Then, and only then, will the Harndue be free of them. When the day dawns that they stand at our gates you will face their King on the battlefield and you will destroy him and his army. And you will make the Harndue the most powerful tribe of all time.'

Tosni felt a shiver run down his spine. He looked at his father's face contorted by his emotion into something Tosni recoiled from.

His mother reached over and squeezed Tosni's hand, 'Aytasnay, when they are at the gates, and ready to attack, you will understand. You will do what you have to do and we will be proud of you.'

'Mother, how can I kill all those people? I hadn't even heard of the Pirous until a few moons ago. I don't think...'

'You will be ready when they arrive,' spat his father. 'Now leave us and think hard on what I have said.'

Back in his room Tosni went to the window which looked east. The plains beyond the boundary wall rippled in the wind looking fresh and green with new growth. Behind them the dark line of forest blurred the horizon. It was from this direction the Pirous were to come. Tosni flung open the casement and breathed in the fresh air trying to clear his head and control his anger. After a while he left the window and sat on the edge of the bed.

Absentmindedly he picked up a book from the pile Hedna had brought him. It was a small and rather thin book compared to most others in the library. Embossed on the old leather cover were the words;

*The Ancient Laws of Magic*
*a guide for the practicing sorcerer*

'There can't be too many Laws if they can squash them all in here!' he muttered turning the book over in his hands, 'But then, considering my parents expect me to kill off a whole army, that sounds about right.' he dropped the book onto the bed and paced the room feeling trapped. Surly there was another way. But who could he ask?

Raven?

Ha!

Hedna then or Elena? He picked up another of the books Elena had selected for him. It was a good deal heavier than the others and was entitled;

*Harnde*
*The History and The Glory*

'Right! Well no doubt I'm meant to add to both!' he grumbled aloud throwing the book back onto the bed with such force the slim, 'Ancient Laws of Magic' bounced onto the floor.

He picked it up and flicked through its meagre contents. There were only four pages of ancient vellum inside the thick outer covers. The first page was so badly stained that he could make little out. He started on the second page and read,

*'..and so, a sorcerer's power is a gift that is neither good nor evil.*

*And while the sorcerer uses it solely for good, so it will remain.*

*But once used for evil, it and the wielder become altogether evil.*

*And the greater the sorcerer's power, and the greater the deed, the greater the evil which will be unleashed.*

*Sorcerer, beware the evil deed cloaked in goodness.*

*It masks your ruin.*

*Yet he who withholds his powers out of weakness, or fear of harm to himself, shall be dammed.*

*For the power is given so it may be wielded.*

*Withholding it in a time of need would be the greatest betrayal of all.'*

Tosni read it again, aloud, *'A sorcerer's power is a gift that is neither good nor evil. And while the sorcerer uses it solely for good, so it will remain.'* Relief washed over him. This seemed to be saying that his power was not going to automatically turn to evil; he had to do something evil first. He skimmed down the words to read the next bit that had caught his eye, *'Yet he who withholds his powers out of weakness, or fear of harm to himself, shall be dammed. For the power is given so it may be wielded and withholding it in a time of need would be the greatest betrayal of all.'*

He swallowed. Was he being weak? Was he just afraid to do what he had to do? Had he found the guidance he sort? This was telling him quite clearly that his powers had been given to him for a purpose and to refuse to use them would be wrong. Yet it also said that to use them for evil would turn him evil. But how was he to know if what he was being asked to do was evil or not? He skimmed quickly through the other pages hoping for more. Maybe there was a simple spell he could perform to allow him to see the right thing to do. But the book offered no solutions. Frustrated and angry he slammed it shut and dropped it onto the bed with the others.

# Chapter Twelve
*The Pirous Army*

Tosni was kept so busy that the next few days flew by. His lessons with Raven were increased, although Raven never asked him to kill again. He was also instructed in the way the Harndue were to draw up battle lines to meet the Pirous. He was shown how each regiment would assemble, taught who their commanders were and what his own role would be and how he was to go about it. The mood of the castle seemed to fluctuate between fear and celebration. By day, the prudent horded food and stabled their animals in the vast caverns cut into the mountain side. Yet in the taverns on an evening, the talk was of victory and an air of excitement spilled out into the surrounding streets like a miasma.

Tosni spent as much time away from the town's people as possible. He was filled with guilt as they bowed and beamed at him convinced he was as set on destroying the Pirous as they were. Shouts of 'Aytasnay, our redeemer' and 'blessings on you Lord Aytasnay' followed him through the streets. Tosni would give a weak smile in return, but escape back into his rooms as soon as he could. He could not celebrate with them. He felt like a coward and a traitor.

As Dunbia predicted, the battle horn was sounded three days later signalling the Pirous had been sighted. Tosni was awake instantly. He leaped out of bed and ran to the eastern window throwing it open. At the edge of the distant forest was a vast army. The sun had just cleared the horizon and it glinted from armour and weapons as the soldiers reformed themselves into battle lines. The bold colours of their tunics were muted by the thinning, early-morning mists. The sounds of raised voices, the clank of armour and the jingle of harness were softened by distance. The columns of men moved swiftly and expertly into their positions. Within a very short time they were still and ready for what was to come. Tosni did not known what he had expected the Pirous army to be like but it certainly wasn't this. They looked proud, even noble and Tosni's heart leapt in his chest at the sight of them. Then it sank, like a stone, into the pit of his stomach. This was his prey, these disciplined, colourful, proud men. This was the army he had been trained to destroy. According to his father it was the reason he had been born. The reason he had been cursed with his powers.

So many lives to be taken.

So many.

He leaned over the sill and vomited.


Tosni pulled on his top and leggings and slumped onto the bed. A knock on the door announced the arrival of Elena. She was followed by Hedna and two other maids. Between them they carried a huge breakfast tray, a jug of steaming water and a pile of clothes.

'Good morning, master Tosni. You heard the trumpets then?' Hedna's dark eyes were bright her face alight with excitement. 'Guessed you would, didn't I Elena. I said 'he'll be up and waiting for us'.'

Elena signalled to the two young maids, 'Just put the clothes and whatnot over there. Then you can leave. Me and Hedna can manage from here.' The girls did as they were asked, then, with shy smiles at Tosni, they left.

Hedna poured the water into a bowl. 'I've got you some nice warm water. But eat first, and then you can wash.'

Tosni looked at the tray Elena had put on the low chest and his stomach clenched in protest. 'I'm not hungry, thanks.'

'Oh, that's just a few nerves. Nothing wrong with that.' Hedna said. 'My old Mama used to say, a few nerves makes a job well done.' Eat a bit, it'll help. You're going to need your strength afore today's out.'

Tosni shook his head and turned away fighting down another wave of nausea. He caught Elena looking at him with an odd expression. 'You don't need to be worrying, master Tosni, she said softly. 'You're more than a match for anything this day can throw at you, mark my words. When the time comes you will do the right thing. And I'm not the only one that believes so neither. Have a little faith in yourself.'

Tosni stared at her. Was he that transparent? Were they all talking about his reluctance to fight? Did they think him a coward?

As if reading his mind Elena shook her head and smiled, 'We don't doubt your bravery. Not for a moment. Now if you don't want to eat, you may as well have a wash and we'll get you into your battle clothes.'

Dressed in the yellow and black of the Harnde tribe, Elena led Tosni to Dunbia and Metalin's rooms. Hedna, still cooing and prattling aimlessly, had left them. 'Don't mind her, my Lord, she means well but can't see any further than right before her nose.'

'Whereas I think you have seer's blood in your veins!' Tosni said absently.

Elena flicked a look over her shoulder looking scared. 'Please sir, not so loud, if it's discovered I'll lose my position.'

'You do have seer's blood?' Tosni whispered

'Yes, but we're not allowed to hold positions in the castle for fear of learning of things we ought not to know.'

Tosni walked on in silence. When this was over he would have a lot of questions for Elena. But at the moment there was only one that seemed important enough to ask.

'Elena, have you seen what is to happen today? Do I... do I kill all those people?'

'I can't say. The only thing you should know is that today you find the peace you're looking for.' She giggled at the horrified look Tosni felt creep over his face. 'No. I don't mean in death. I mean in life, true life.'

'What life?'

But Elena had already knocked at the white doors.

There was only his father and Raven in the room. Tosni looked quickly around for sign of his mother but she was not there.

'Aytasnay, join us.' Dunbia waved him into the room and Elena made a hasty exit. 'Raven has nothing but praise for your gifts and your ability to use them. You are going to make us proud.'

Dunbia's face was flushed and he strode around the room hands on hips. Raven stood leaning against the stone arch of one of the windows. His arms were crossed and his eyes fixed on Tosni.

'How do you feel now the great day is here?' his father asked.

Tosni swallowed, how did he feel? He loathed himself and his powers. He was terrified at what he was being asked to do, but worst of all he was trapped by the dawning realization that he could not let any harm come to the Harndue. He would kill if he had to, to save them.

'I am ready.'

'Good. Good,' Dunbia beamed at him. 'What did I tell you? Didn't I say you would be ready for the kill when the day came? Today will be the beginning of a new era for the Harndue and you will be the one to bring it about. I will accompany you onto the battlefield with a score of our finest archers and another of armed horsemen. We will need no more than that. Raven is to stay here as back up if it is needed but we are sure that you are more than capable of destroying their army without help. The stories of your powers have obviously reached even their arrogant ears as they have assembled their best. Have you seen them?' he said, pulling Tosni to the window. 'Hah! Even their best will be no match for you. A thousand of their finest will be destroyed today and the remnants, if there are any, will be scattered far and wide to be picked off at our leisure. Then we will march on their city and raze it to the ground.' Dunbia was pacing around the room now, his face flushed by his excitement and spittle spraying from his lips. 'Every male over ten summers will be killed of course. But the women and children will serve us. The high and mighty Pirous will be annihilated.'

Tosni tuned away from the window and clutched the back of a chair for support. The room swam around him and he had to will himself to remain standing.

Dunbia did not seem to notice and spun around to face the watching sorcerer. 'What say you, Raven?'

Raven's black eyes slid from Tosni to Dunbia and he dipped his head in acknowledgement. 'It will be as you say, my Lord.'

'Aytasnay?'

Unable to speak Tosni nodded.

'Good. Go now and prepare. We ride at noon.'

Feeling as though the world were spinning around him, Tosni left the room. His mother was waiting for him in the passage-way. She stroked his cold white cheek. 'Know this, Aytasnay,' she whispered quickly, 'whatever happens today you are blood of my blood and I will always be proud of you.' Before he could persuade his numb lips to form an answer she had turned and was gone.

# Chapter Thirteen
*Face to Face*

Tosni stood looking out of the window of his room while Elena braided his hair into a black and yellow thong.

'Elena, you said that today I would find peace, what did you mean by that?'

'I've told you all I can, my Lord, and probable more than I should.' She finished the braid and patted into place. 'But, perhaps there is something I can say and hopefully, in the future, you can take some comfort from it.' Elena paused and turning Tosni around she looked into his eyes. 'You should know this, my Lord, those of us with the ability to see, understand you better even than you do yourself. We know you will do the right thing and we revere you for it and wish you joy. Now I must go.'

'What? Elena I don't...' But Elena had already left the room almost knocking over the page carrying Tosni's armour in her haste.

Tosni stood silent as the page fastened the metal breast plate over the black and yellow tunic. Elena's words made no sense to him. What did they know? And who were 'they'? Did she mean the seers? What had they seen? What choice could he possibly have? If he did nothing he and the Harndue would die. If he acted then the Pirous would die. And not just the army but all Pirous, everywhere. The page held out leather gauntlets for Tosni to slip his hands into. Tosni shook his head, he was going to need his hands. It was how he directed his power. He also refused to wear the helmet. He did not want the close fitting helm impairing his hearing or vision. As soon as he was dressed the page led him through the castle to the immense courtyard and the assembled archers and knights. The shifting sea of yellow and black parted and Dunbia, mounted on his horse, rode over to him.

'Come, Aytasnay, show the Pirous how powerful we have become.'

Tosni became aware they were waiting for him to climb into a litter.

Dunbia saw his hesitation and said, 'We want you to be visible. We want them to be in no doubt you are with us.'

On legs that no longer felt like his own Tosni forced himself to walk over to the litter and climb in. He sat stiffly on the small throne grasping the carved arms. As the soldiers hoisted the litter up onto their shoulders Tosni swallowed hard at the rising bile in his throat. The gates into the city swung open to the sound of horses' feet clattering restlessly on the flagged courtyard. The smell of their hot bodies and leather saddlery drifted up to him. The assembled crowds cheered as the mounted knights led the way through the gates into the city. The way to the outer gates was lined with cheering town people waving yellow and black flags. Cries of 'Lord Aytasnay, our saviour' spread like a wave as they moved forward. At the outer wall the gates opened onto the enclosed fields. Tosni stared straight ahead as the litter bearers left the shadowy streets and walked into the glare of the midday sun. He squinted in the dazzling sunlight. The cheering crowd were left behind in the safety of the city. As the gates swung shut their cheering stopped and they raced to find vantage points higher up on the cliff face. A soft breeze ruffled the grasses in the empty paddocks. The sound of horses' snorting and gently mouthing their bits drifted around him while above him a bird trilled its joy of life. Everything was calm. There was no sign of the bloodshed that was to come. Tosni's heart hammered in his chest. As he raised his eyes to look at the silent army spread out at the edge of the forest, his blood rose and pounded in his ears. He gripped the arms of the throne until his fingers were numb. Dunbia was at the side of the litter now and his voice was sharp with excitement. It pulled Tosni's attention back from the arrayed army.

Raising his arm in the air Dunbia yelled, 'Forward,'

The archers moved off, parting as they went so that the litter carrying Tosni could join their ranks. Behind them came the mounted knights. Holding this formation they passed the neatly fenced off fields and approached the gates which opened onto the outer plain and the Pirous. Four soldiers leaped from the shadow of the wall and swung the enormous gates open. Tosni and his escort passed through them.

Once through the gates Dunbia dropped back behind the litter. The litter bearers moved Tosni forward to take the lead. He knew he was being displayed, held up as a trophy. As a warning. The Harndue wanted the arrayed army to see him. They wanted the Pirous to be afraid at the mere sight of him. Then, they wanted the Pirous to die. Tosni breathed deeply, willing himself not to retch again.

The heat of the day hung over him like a cloying blanket. The gentle breeze had no power to cool him. It did not even stir the enemy's banners. The soldiers red tunics were covered by silver armour. Red cloaks were fastened over one shoulder exposing their fighting arm and weapons. White plumes sprung from each mounted captain's helm. The army stood silent but for the jingle of harness and the occasional stomp of horses' feet. If they were afraid, if they had heard of Tosni's powers, his ability to kill with a wave of his hand, they showed no sign of it. As Tosni approached, he picked out their King. He was mounted on a huge Chestnut horse and wore a red helm adorned with a white feather. The morning sun glinted off his red breastplate and over one shoulder was slung a red cloak. A standard bearer on a big bay horse stood by his side, the standard hung limp in the barely moving air. Tosni knew he was to direct his power against this man, the King and leader of the Pirous army. The brother of Metalin. He looked so proud, so noble... He is the man who stole his sister's child from the cradle and condemned him to years of misery, Tosni reminded himself forcefully.

Tosni's party came to a halt some hundred meters in front of the enemy. In response, the Pirous King and a small escort peeled away from the red clad army and rode out to meet them. Tosni watched transfixed as the King approached. The standard, swaying with the movement of the bearer's horse, flashed red and green. The thrum of the horse's hooves and clatter of armour sounded loud on the silent field.

'Now, Aytasnay,' Dunbia whispered from behind. 'Strike now while your target is clear. The rest will be easily picked off later.'

As if in a nightmare he couldn't escape, Tosni raised his hand. He felt the power rise freely from deep inside him and loathed it. Ravens teaching had shown him how to access his power at will but each time he did he felt as if he were reaching into an everlasting well of death and destruction. The approaching King reined in at the sight of Tosni's raised hand. Then, with no more than a moment's hesitation, he dismounted and began to walk toward the litter accompanied only by his unhorsed standard bearer.

'Now, Tosni, strike now before he can weave his evil magic,' hissed Dunbia.

The helmed King stopped a few feet from them. Tosni's hand remained raised, he could feel the energy tingle between his outstretched fingers.

'What are you waiting for? Strike him down.' Dunbia shouted. He had rode to the side of the litter and stared at Tosni. Tosni stared back and as he looked into Dunbia's eyes he saw a spark of fear flicker deep within them. It kindled an answering spark within him. This is wrong, he thought, and Dunbia knows it. A verse from the old book of law came into his mind. And as clear as if it were being whispered in his ear he heard the words,

*Sorcerer, beware the evil deed cloaked in goodness. It masks your ruin.*

Is that what this was? An evil deed that had been cloaked in goodness? But how? The Pirous leader was an evil person. He had stolen Tosni from his parents when Tosni was no more than a baby, intending to use his powers for evil. But the whispering in his ear continued,

*Yet he who withholds his powers out of weakness, or fear of harm to himself, shall be dammed.*
*For the power is given so it may be wielded and withholding it in a time of need would be the greatest betrayal of all.*

How was he to judge which this was? Was he being weak? Was he just afraid of doing what had to be done? Holding the power in his hand he turned his mind to the litter bearers, forcing them to lower the litter. As they did so he heard Dunbia scream, 'Archers, release.'

With barely an effort Tosni froze the arrows in the bows and the archers where they stood.

'I have to know,' he shouted to Dunbia as he climbed down from the lowered litter, 'I have to understand.'

'He has bewitched you as I warned he would. You are being controlled by him. Strike him down before it is too late,' Dunbia screeched.

But Tosni did not strike. The only thing he was sure of at that moment was that the tall King standing quietly before him was not controlling him. Tosni knew that had the King even attempted such a thing he would be instantly aware of it, and Tosni would kill him. He walked toward the King trying to catch a glimpse of his eyes through the visor of his helm. The king did not move. But Dunbia, also on foot now, drew his sword and ran with a scream of rage at the King. Instantly the King drew his sword in response and braced himself for the attack. Behind the King, Tosni saw the Pirous archers raise their bows ready to defend their King and he knew he could delay no longer. He lifted his hand again, this time to kill. But as the King swung his sword to parry Dunbia's blow, Tosni caught sight of an ornament glinting on his shoulder. The familiar shape and colours made Tosni's heart leap. At the last possible instant Tosni turned his death strike into a freezing spell.

The King and Dunbia stood immobile, the armies were suspended in time while Tosni stared at the King's torn brooch. The same blue sky the same green hills and, in the foreground, the head and shoulders of a red lion. The breath caught in Tosni's throat. He felt as if a metal band were tightening around his chest restricting his breathing. With trembling fingers he took out his treasure staring at it as if he had never really seen it before. The familiar blue, green and red shone back at him. He reached out and held it to the broken ornament on the King's shoulder. The two halves fitted together perfectly. Tosni felt the warm air flood back into his lungs as he stared at the two halves of the brooch, reunited after eleven years

# Chapter Fourteen
*The Brooch*

As Tosni stared at the brooch, trying to take in the implications of what he saw. The world around him faded into darkness. The armies, the plain, the forest and castle were swallowed by the blackness and only Tosni and the immobile King remained. A fierce light exploded from the ugly gash where the two halves of the brooch were reunited. Tosni flung his arm over his eyes and when he lowered it again a picture was forming in the centre of the light. He stood transfixed as the picture slowly came into focus. A grassy bank, a stream, bushes heavy with white blossoms. With unfathomable logic Tosni knew that what he saw no longer existed. It was no more than an echo of a time from years ago. Suddenly he was wrenched off his feet. With a shout of alarm he was pulled into the picture spinning head over heels then landing with a bone jarring thud on his feet. He steadied himself and looked around. The battle field, the armies, Dunbia, the King, everything was gone. He was in the picture; drawn back through time. A spectator of the past. He was close to the stream. He could hear its gentle music as it jostled over its pebbly bed. The sweet scent of the white flowering bushes tickled his nostrils. Everything was softly blurred as if the passing of time had shrouded everything in a fine mist. A man's voice came from the nearby bushes. Tosni ducked into the long grass and watched a red-haired man came out of the trees holding a small child by the hand. The man was obviously of noble birth. His heavy leggings and velvet doublet were covered by a thick fur lined cloak. The child was very young and still unsteady on his feet and his father supported his wobbly, uneven gait. As they approached him Tosni sprang to his feet.

'Who are you?' he asked, but the man did not answer. He continued to talk to the baby, passing close to where Tosni stood.

'Where is this?' Tosni said, a little louder.

Still the man did not look at him or answer. 'He can't see me,' he thought, 'and he obviously can't hear me. But,' he reminded himself, 'if this is the past then I'm not really here. I'm just watching shadows, memories. But why am I here? And how can I get back to the battle field?'

Tosni watched as the man bent at the edge of the river to help the child choose a stone. As he did so Tosni saw a broach pinned to his cloak. He caught his breath. But the strange mist blurred its outline. He had to get closer. Tosni walked towards the man and child to get a better look but that moment three men rushed from the bushes nearby. Unlike the nobleman these men were dressed roughly. Two of them sported an ill matched assortment of leather armour, one with a dented helm. The third wore a coarse grey-brown tunic. The red-haired man pushed the child behind him. Shielding him with his body he drew his sword. The man with the helm rushed in and took a sword thrust to his belly. As he crumpled to the ground the second leapt to grab the child. A dagger appeared in the father's hand as if from nowhere and he swung it viciously catching this second attacker a cruel slash to his upper arm. The man howled in pain and backed off. Tosni thought at first that the nobleman would fight his attackers off, but, as he drew his sword from the belly of the dead man, the third man, the one in the grey-brown tunic leapt forward. Tosni stared at him and his stomach turned over. He knew this man. There was no mistaking that hated face, screwed up though it was in vicious enjoyment. Halon! Anger welled inside of Tosni and he raised his hand to strike the man down, to stop him from doing what he knew was to come. But no magic sparkled from his fingers. No well of boiling energy was there to be drawn from. He was helpless. Halon was swinging what looked like a rope with a stone tied to each end. The red-haired man was unaware of this new threat as he had turned at the sudden, terrified scream of the child as it lurched into the stream. Tosni shouted a warning and ran forward but neither Halon nor the man heard him. The nobleman pulled the child to safety then turned to face his attackers again but Halon had already released the rope. Tosni reached to pluck the stones from the air but the rope passed through his fingers as if they were no more than smoke. One of the stones smashed into the side of the nobleman's head, the rope wound around his neck and shoulders and blood oozed over his face as he stumbled to his knees. He groped blindly for his sword which had been knocked from his hand. Halon stepped forward and kicked the sword away then pushed the stunned, bleeding man to the ground. The man rolled and clutched the child to his chest curling around him in a desperate effort to keep him safe. But instead of finishing him off, as Tosni expected him to, Halon retreated to where his wounded comrade lay. He helped him to his feet and then they kept their distance, watching, sword drawn. Only then did a fourth man step from the shadows and Tosni knew him at once. It was Dunbia.

Dunbia went to the fallen man and tore the screaming, blood stained child from his arms. The father made a desperate attempt to regain his feet and get to the boy. He had managed to pull himself to one knee when Dunbia drew his dagger. With a twisted smile he brought the dagger down in a vicious arc. As the knife slashed through the air Tosni was unaware if the scream that filled his ears was his own or Dunbia's. The dagger sliced through the man's cheek before plunging into his chest. Dunbia turned and handed the screaming child to the ragged Halon. From the pouch on his belt he took a handful of gold coin and threw them on the ground at Halon's feet.

'Keep the child alive and you shall receive payment every fourth moon. I want him back safe and whole at the start of his thirteenth summer or you will pay the price.'

Halon picked up the coin and strode away with the screaming baby under his arm. His companion followed. Dunbia turned back to the red-haired nobleman who lay unmoving as his blood stained the ground. He kicked him savagely.

'May you die slowly, Antone.'

The injured man rolled onto his back and as he did so Tosni saw his brooch clearly. Only now it was no longer whole. It was jagged and torn.

# Chapter Fifteen
## *The Truth*

The mist began to swirl around Tosni, spinning him off his feet and with a blast of colour and heat he was back on the battlefield. For a second or two Tosni could have been as frozen in time as the two armies. He stood, arm out stretched, staring at the brooch on the King's shoulder. Certainty coursed through him but he had to have proof. Slowly, holding his breath, he reached out and unfurled the King's standard. A red lion on a field of green beneath a blue sky. He exhaled and as he did so felt a warm tear trickle down his cheek. He brushed it away with shaking hands and eased the red helm from the King's head. A coil of red hair, neatly braided, fell to his shoulders. Green eyes stared unseeingly toward his enemy. And there, across his cheek, was a ragged scar.

Tosni stared at the King.

'Father?'

He felt the word form in his mind and knew that at last he was face to face with his real father. And he knew without any doubt that he was the boy in the vision; the boy the King had defended so desperately. Dunbia had stolen him. Dunbia had given him to Halon. It was Dunbia who had taken him from his family for this one terrible task; to destroy his father and his people. Anger surged through Tosni then tightened around his innards like a snake. Dropping the helm he spun about to face Dunbia. Dunbia was frozen in the middle of his charge at the king his face was contorted with fear and rage. His sword was high, stilled in its killing blow. Tosni clenched his fists in an effort to control his furious anger. He wanted to crush Dunbia, to lash out and destroy him as Dunbia had so carefully taught him to. But Tosni knew that if he did that then Dunbia would still have won. Tosni's powers would still be turned irrevocable to evil. He would become a threat to everyone. The Harndue. The Pirous. His father. Everyone would be in danger from him. He screamed his frustration feeling his throat burn with the depth of his rage. Raising his arm he swept it in front of him as if sweeping away the sight of Dunbia and his guard. When he lowered it the Harndue were gone, the plain before him was empty. From the distant castle he heard the trumpets blare their warning. He breathed deeply, trying to calm himself and hanging on to the bleak satisfaction that he had overcome Dunbia's training. Despite Dunbia's best efforts, Tosni had not killed. He had confined the Harndue to the castle. Temporarily. A few days no more, but it would be long enough for the Pirous to be far away before the spell broke and the castle relinquished its hold on the captives.

He took a last deep, steadying breath before turning to the king, his father. As he looked into the scared face all his hopes rekindled. His life would be different from now on. Maybe this time he could find happiness. He was no longer so childish to think it would be perfect but surly there would at least be joy. He suddenly understood what Elena had been trying to tell him. Elena had known what was to happen today yet she had wished him joy. He drew comfort from that and the knowledge he had not harmed her people, despite what they had done to him. He had controlled his powers and he had used them only for good, despite Dunbia and Raven's best efforts to make them evil. He stared at the King, savouring the moment, knowing that finally he was about to find out who, and what, he truly was.

He passed his hand before the King and his entourage and stepped nimbly aside to avoid the King's blade as it completed its arc. Arrows arched overhead onto the now empty plain. The King stood ready to defend himself from an enemy that was no longer there. Slowly he relaxed his sword arm and turned to Tosni. Tosni watched his gaze move from Tosni's face to the discarded helm at his feet.

'Aytasnay? You know me?'

'My name is Tosni. But yes, father, I finally know you.'

His father grinned and pulled him into a crushing hug against his metal breast plate.

'My son. It really is you. Until the rumours reached us we believed you were dead. Not even Venton could find trace of you.'

'Dunbia wanted me so I could be trained to kill you,' Tosni said flatly.

'I knew why you were stolen, but I also knew that should the day come when we would face each other on the battle field, you would not kill your people.'

Tosni wondered if the King would ever know how close he had come to being proven wrong.

'But how did you recognize me? Surely Dunbia did not tell you the truth?'

Tosni shook his head. 'No. He's told me nothing but lies.' He held out his half of broach and pointed to the brooch on the King's shoulder. 'This was how I knew.'

'You have it still?'

Tosni nodded.

'But...' The king looked about as if realizing the field before him was empty, 'where are the Harndue?'

'Confined to the castle. For now at least.'

The King put his arm around Tosni's shoulders. 'Come your mother is waiting to welcome you along with others you may be pleased to see.'

His father returned to his horse and mounted. Tosni climbed up behind and they led the way off the battlefield and back to the camp of the Pirous. As they rode his father told him how the sorcerer Venton had searched for him after he was stolen but how Tosni had been shielded from view leading Venton to think him dead. How, by the time his father had recovered from his wounds, the trail was long cold and impossible to follow. How, when Tosni's powers had begun to show themselves, Venton had realized he was still alive but was unable to pinpoint where he was.

'It was only when the Harndue took you back and began to train you that the cloak of deceit fell away. Then Venton saw the truth of what had happened all those years ago and where you had been hidden until you came into your power. As soon as we knew for certain where you were, I came to get you back,' his father said. 'There were some who said I was foolhardy, meeting you in battle, but I knew my son could never kill his people.'

Tosni did not answer. They had come to the bottom of a low rise and people were gathered at the top of the hill cheering them home. He held his breath as they cantered up the rise to the camp. Tents were gathered in orderly rows. The King slowed his horse to a walk and they strode through the jubilant crowd to the centre of the camp. People were cheering, patting Tosni's legs and grabbing his hands as he passed in welcome. Then the crowd opened up and fell silent. In the centre of the clearing was a small fair haired woman. She stood hands clasped to her mouth staring up at him. Tosni slid to the ground and took a hesitant step toward her.

'Mother?'

She nodded. Face wet with tears she held out her arms and he went to her. She hugged him, crying openly. Her soft perfume filled his nostrils. The crowds roared their approval. Then his father was next to them gently unwrapping his mother's arms.

'There is someone else I think you might be pleased to see Tosni. Come, look.'

He turned Tosni around and there, with Salif balanced precariously on one skinny hip, was Willem.

'Willem! Salif!' Tosni rushed toward them. Willem was blushing furiously but at the sound of Tosni's voice Salif buried her face in Willem's jerkin.

'Salif?' Tosni said uncertainly. Salif lifted her head and stared at Tosni, her dark eyes round, her face very serious. Then as if suddenly recognizing him, she screamed in delight bouncing up and down on Willem's hip with her arms outstretched. Tosni snatched her up spinning her round and round sharing her delight. When he stopped Willem was standing sheepishly by.

'You are a sorcerer then?' he said, his voice only just audible above the noise of the crowd.

The smile slid from Tosni's face. 'Yeah I am, but it's not like the villagers say it is. I mean...'

''S okay. I know. We've been here a couple of weeks and well, I understand loads more than I did.' He nodded at Salif, 'She looks happy to see you.'

Salif was rubbing her open mouth on Tosni's cheek in a parody of a kiss.

'Thanks for taking care of her, Willem, she looks fine.'

Willem shrugged, ''S okay,' he said again, 'It was a bit like having a baby sister after a while. When it got that Kavnen didn't care if Salif was with her or not we took her in. At least that was until the soldiers turned up with gold. Then she was quick enough to claim her back of course!'

'Did you get your cloak and boots back? I sent them with Dunbia's men to give you. How come they didn't bring me Salif?'

'Dunbia's men? No one came until your father did. He came himself with half his army. You should of seen it Tosni, they road through the village demanding that the son of the King be brought to them. But instead of going out to see what all the fuss was about, everyone ran and hid. But I guessed who they wanted and I went to speak to the leader and tell him you had left, that you had gone south to look for your father. And you know what he said?'

Tosni shook his head.

'He said 'I am his father and I won't rest until he is back with me.' Then of course I realized he was the king and I decided I had better shut up but he got me to tell him all I knew. He wanted to know about your life in the village and Kavnen and Salif. But most of all he wanted to know where you had gone, so I told him about the parchment and how Kavnen had put you out and how you'd had to leave Salif behind. When he said he would take Salif with him that was when Kavnen appeared and demanded payment. He asked if I would ride with him to care for Salif and to make you feel more at home when you returned. 'Course by this time my father had come out of the cottage after me and he heard. It didn't take that much persuading before he said, yes. So here I am.'

The king came over and put an arm on each of their shoulders. 'Willem's father has given his permission for him to stay with us a few weeks longer which will give you plenty time to catch up. But for now, Tosni, I think that you should get to know your people. We have waited a long time for this.'

Tosni found himself grinning again. He was home at last. And with Salif on his hip and Willem by his side he allowed his father and mother to lead him away to be formally presented to his people.

## The End

Thank you for reading The Lost Sorcerer. If you have enjoyed this novella then please consider writing a short review on Amazon. A good review will help others to find this book.


Also by Maureen Murrish

The Dragon World Series;
The Bonding Crystal
The Missing Link


Keep up with new releases and items of interest on

http://maureen-murrish.blogspot.co.uk/

5988285R00053

Printed in Great Britain
by Amazon.co.uk, Ltd.,
Marston Gate.